Sophie's Secret

Other books in the growing Faithgirlz!™ library

Best Friends Bible

The Sophie Series

Sophie's World (Book One)
Sophie and the Scoundrels (Book Three)
Sophie's Irish Showdown (Book Four)
Sophie's First Dance? (Book Five)
Sophie's Stormy Summer (Book Six)

Nonfiction

No Boys Allowed: Devotions for Girls

Check out www.faithgirlz.com

faiThGirLz!™

Sophie's Secret
Nancy Rue

Zonderkidz

Zonder**kidz**.

The children's group of Zondervan

www.zonderkidz.com

Requests for information should be addressed to:
Zonderkidz, 5300 Patterson Ave. SE
Grand Rapids, Michigan 49530

ISBN: 0-310-70757-9

Library of Congress Cateloging-in-Publication application has been made.

Published in association with the literary agency of Alive Communications, Inc., 7680 Goddard Street, Suite 200, Colorado Springs, CO 80920.

Photography: Synergy Photographic/Brad Lampe
Illustrations: Grace Chen Design & Illustration
Art direction/design: Michelle Lenger
Interior design: Susan Ambs
Interior composition: Pamela J. L. Eicher

Printed in the United States of America

04 05 06 07 08/❖DC/5 4 3 2

So we fix our eyes not on what is seen, but on what is unseen. For what is seen is temporary, but what is unseen is eternal.

— 2 Corinthians 4:18

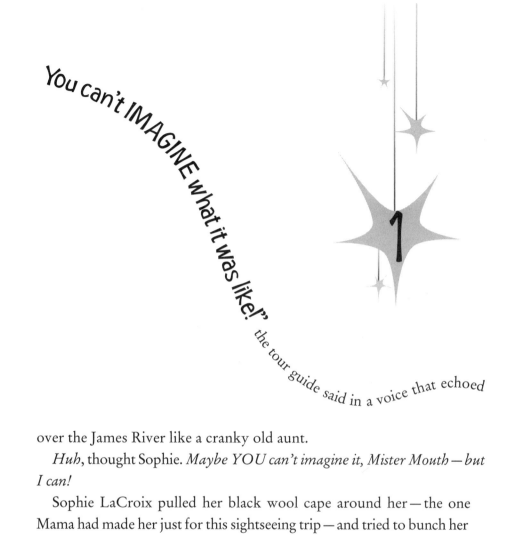

You can't IMAGINE what it was like!" the tour guide said in a voice that echoed

over the James River like a cranky old aunt.

Huh, thought Sophie. *Maybe YOU can't imagine it, Mister Mouth — but I can!*

Sophie LaCroix pulled her black wool cape around her — the one Mama had made her just for this sightseeing trip — and tried to bunch her long, not-quite-blonde-not-quite-brown hair into the hood to muffle Mr. Mouth's voice. How was she supposed to concentrate on the delicious realness of Jamestown Island, with this guy barging into the quiet, telling her that she, Sophie LaCroix, "-couldn't imagine?"

Imagining is my specialty, she wanted to inform him. *Have YOU ever imagined YOURself back in the eighteenth century, acted it out, and made a film of it?* Sophie sniffed. *Probably NOT.*

She edged away from the guide and gazed across the river. In the film they'd just watched in the Visitors' Center — well, SHE and Mama had actually watched it while her thirteen-year-old sister Lacie and Aunt Bailey had made fun of the narrator talking like he had a chip bag clip on his nose — the narrator's voice had described the river as "a salty brine at high tide and a blend of slime and filth at low." Sophie wanted to repeat this to her best friend, Fiona, back at school, and maybe they could start saying that about the Poquoson River in THEIR town. It would sound so cool. So would "the drear dark sky" — which did stretch over the river on that day-after-Thanksgiving and slowly soak them with drizzle. Mama had wanted her to put on a plastic poncho, but that would totally ruin the effect of the cape.

Besides, Sophie thought, *I'm sure Captain John Smith didn't have a plastic raincoat back in 1607.* No, this experience had to be as real as she could make it — so she and Fiona and Kitty could develop their next movie about it.

Because, of course, that's what they — the Corn Flakes — would have to do as soon as Thanksgiving vacation was over. A "cheerless sky" and the possibility of cruel diseases "such as swellings, fluxes, and burning fevers" like the film had described: that stuff was too good to waste. Sophie stretched out her hands to the river.

Antoinette called silently to God to help her know the secrets that lay at the slimy, filthy river bottom. Antoinette's heart began to pound as she found herself at the brink of some new mission — some fascinating adventure — some brilliant endeavor that would make Papa see once and for all that she was worthy of his honor and respect —

"Soph — what are you doing?"

Sophie felt a heavy hand on her shoulder, and she had to scurry back from Antoinette's world to focus up at her father. He was towering over her, and nobody could tower like way-tall Daddy with his broad, I-used-to-be-a-football-star shoulders and his sharp blue eyes, so unlike Sophie's soft brown ones. In fact, Sophie always thought that if somebody lined up a dozen fathers and asked a stranger to pick out which one was hers, they'd never get the right one.

"We're all headed up to the fort," Daddy said.

"Can't I just stay and look at the river for a couple more minutes?" Sophie said.

Daddy shook his big dark head. "No, because next thing I know you'll be in it. We're working as a team today."

Sophie muttered an "okay" and tried to wriggle her shoulder out of his hand, but he had the Daddy Grip on it.

"No way, Soph," he said. "I don't want a repeat of that Williamsburg thing."

Sophie didn't remind him that she had grown WAY up since THAT happened back in September. *What would be the point?* she thought as she broke into a jog to keep up with him. *He thinks I'm the biggest ditz in the universe and he always will. And it's SO not fair!*

"I wish you would've let me bring my video camera," she said.

Daddy gave a grunt. "Uh-huh—then I'd have to keep you on a leash." He stopped about six feet from a statue where Mama, her little brother Zeke, Lacie, and Aunt Bailey and Uncle Preston were gathered.

Wonderful, Sophie thought. *He's going to give me a lecture right here where they can all hear.* She wished she'd never asked the question.

At least Daddy squatted down in front of her, so his voice wouldn't boom down to her tiny height, but he still didn't let go of her shoulder. It was all she could do not to squirm.

"Look, we've had this discussion before," he said.

Yeah, about sixty bajillion times, Sophie thought.

"Everything is not always all about you," he went on.

It NEVER is!

"We're here to do what Aunt Bailey and Uncle Preston want to do, because they're our guests. I don't think that includes standing there watching you stare at the river for an hour, dreaming up trouble."

Sophie straightened her thin shoulders under Daddy's hand. "I was starting an idea for our next film."

"Well, take notes or something." Daddy stood up. "Are you going to stay with the team, or do I have to hold your hand like a little kid? That would be pretty embarrassing for an eleven-year-old."

That was actually a tough question. Sophie did NOT want to be on any kind of "team" with her own sister, much less her aunt and uncle. But the thought of trailing behind her father all day was worse. She gave a sigh from her heels that blew the little wisps of hair on her forehead. It wasn't wasted on Daddy.

"Don't be a drama queen about it," he said, his eyes narrowed. "Just think of it as taking a hit for the team." He nodded toward the statue. "Let's go."

Sophie waited until he finally let go of her shoulder, and then she squared herself off again and headed toward the "team."

Antoinette tossed back her long, luxurious hair and put on a smile. She couldn't let Papa take away the chance to pay her respects to her ancestor, Captain John Smith. He wasn't French like she was, of course, but she thought of him as her forefather because he, like her, had been a pioneer, a taker of risks, a person who stood up against things more evil than good —

"Oh wow — he was a total BABE!"

Sophie glared at Lacie.

"I mean, look at that BODY," Lacie said. She was gaping up at the statue.

Aunt Bailey sidled up next to Lacie. "That's what I'M talkin' about."

Five-year-old Zeke furrowed his little dark brows at Aunt Bailey. "WHAT are you talkin' about?" he said.

Mama cocked her head, all curly with frosted hair, and gave Sophie's aunt a hard look. "Thank you, Bailey," she said.

Aunt Bailey covered her very-red lips with her hand — with its nails all squared off and white at the tips — and giggled in Lacie's direction. Although Aunt Bailey was OLD, like probably thirty, Sophie thought she acted like she was Lacie's age.

"That's John Smith, Z," Daddy said to Zeke. "You remember him from *Pocahontas?*"

"Oh, yeah," Zeke said. He cocked his head just the way Mama did, though his hair was dark like Daddy's, and it stood straight up in coarse, little spikes on his head. "Did they get married?"

"Nah," Daddy said. "They might have gone out a few times, but she married somebody else."

"She married John Rolfe, Daddy," Sophie said. "And I'm SURE she never went on a date with Captain John Smith."

Uncle Preston gave Daddy a nudge with his elbow. "Silly you," he said to him.

Then Daddy gave one of those only-one-side-of-his-mouth-going-up smiles that made Sophie want to punch something. *He might as well just come right out and SAY I'm a little know-it-all,* Sophie thought. *Because that's what he thinks.*

"Watch your tone, Sophie," Daddy said.

WHAT tone? Sophie thought. *I was just sharing information!*

"All right, folks, now if you'll just follow me," Mr. Mouth was saying. "I'm going to take you to the 1607 James Fort site. I think you'll be fascinated by what I have to tell you." He puffed up his chest.

"Now, the question many folks ask me is why do we need to dig up remnants of a civilization that no longer exists?"

"That would be MY question," Lacie muttered to Aunt Bailey. They rolled their eyes in unison.

"Here is the best answer I can give you," Mr. Mouth went on. "The present is better understood when viewed through the lenses of the past — "

Sophie jerked her head around, so that her face was sideways in the hood. Even before she could straighten it out, her mind was teeming.

The lenses of the past! she thought. *The lenses of my camera — that's what they are: "the lenses of the past."*

She really did wish she could take notes — although she was pretty sure she would remember a gem like THAT. Fiona was going to be so impressed.

Sophie stood on a low concrete wall so she could get a better of view of Mr. Mouth. He was now shouting like Lacie's soccer coach, but at least he was finally saying something she wanted to hear.

"That's why it's so significant for archaeologists here at Jamestown to find, for instance, the remains of the fort, " he said, "because it was the center of their life, and this is where they set the precedents for our representative government and legal code."

Sophie didn't know what "precedents" were, but she was sure Fiona would. She stood on her tiptoes to see where Mr. Mouth was now pointing. There were several men wearing hard hats and very dirty clothes, down on their hands and knees, making tiny digs in the dirt with pointed instruments that looked like pens.

"You can see how precise the techniques are," Mr. Mouth said. "But this is the way they discovered the rest of the palisade of the fort. It's called a trenching technique. They're following the white blocks in the ground where they think the palisades were."

"Whatever," Lacie mumbled. Aunt Bailey, of course, nodded. Sophie moved a few more inches away from them on top of the low wall and craned her neck to see the map Mr. Mouth was holding.

"We know where to dig for PHYSICAL evidence — such as building ruins and artifacts — by using the DOCUMENTARY evidence we find. This is a map left by one of the secretaries of the first General Assembly, giving the measurements!"

Mr. Mouth was so delighted with THAT piece of information, he sprayed the people who were standing directly in front of him with enthusiastic spit.

"Gross me out," Lacie whispered to Aunt Bailey.

"We might need those plastic ponchos after all," Aunt Bailey whispered back.

Mama turned and gave Lacie a don't-be-disrespectful look. Sophie would have taken a minute to enjoy that if she hadn't wanted to hear every word Mr. Mouth was saying. She decided to call him Mr. Messenger instead.

He's like a messenger of knowledge from the past, she thought. She KNEW Fiona would be impressed with THAT.

"These archaeologists have uncovered over 350 thousand artifacts dating to the first half of the seventeenth century," Mr. Messenger said. "They have even excavated two large trash pits."

"They dug through the *garbage*?" Lacie said.

This time it didn't come out in a whisper, and Mr. Messenger turned to her with wide eyes, as if he were overjoyed that she'd asked that question.

"Yes, young lady!" he said. "You would be amazed what we can learn about a society from its refuse. In fact, well-preserved trash is a Jamestown treasure!"

Sophie made a mental note of that. Lacie turned to Aunt Bailey and wrinkled her nose.

"I don't think I'd want to know THAT bad," she murmured.

"As you can see," Mr. Messenger said, "they are still working. Where I'm going to take you next, they are excavating what may have been a graveyard."

"This just keeps getting better and better," Aunt Bailey whispered. "First old garbage, now dead bodies."

"And then we'll watch the further excavation of a well," Mr. Messenger continued. "They've already found a metal armor breastplate — "

"Now THAT's a bra," Aunt Bailey said behind her hand to Lacie. "Speaking of bras, we need to go shopping. I know you're wearing the wrong size right now."

Sophie could feel her face going crimson. She checked out her parents to see if they were hearing all this, but Mama was deep in conversation with one of the archaeologists, and Daddy was watching Mama, his arms folded and his head bent toward Uncle Preston.

"What do you want to bet Lynda is at this moment giving that guy directions to our home?" Sophie heard Daddy say. "The woman never meets a stranger."

Mr. Messenger was winding up his explanation before they moved on, and Sophie was now having a harder time focusing on him with all those other conversations going on around her. She leaned out just a tiny bit more.

"When we go into the tent where the archaeologists are working on the well site," Mr. Messenger said, "you will see them using very small trowels to scrape one eighth of an inch of earth at a time and then sweep it into five gallon buckets. All that dirt goes through a screen — "

"Uh-oh," Daddy said to Uncle Preston. "There go all my buckets. Lynda will be down here tomorrow with ten of them and a half a dozen gardening shovels."

Daddy! Sophie wanted to shout at him. *I can't concentrate!*

She leaned out just a little more — and suddenly she was on the ground, tumbling down the incline toward the river.

She tried to grab onto something to stop herself, but she was tangled up in her cape, and half the hood was covering her face.

Arms flailing, she knew she had to be within inches of the water, and all she could think was, *If I fall in, I'm going to be in SO much trouble!*

And then something stopped her, and Sophie clung to it with both cape-entangled arms. With a jerk of her neck, she got the hood off her face and found herself looking up at Mr. Messenger. She was hanging onto his legs.

It was the closest she had been to him, and now she could see that his eyes were twinkling.

"No swimming allowed, missy," he said.

He gave her a grin and a hand to haul herself up with. She dusted off her cape, and then she curtsied.

"Thank you, kind sir," she said.

He dipped into a deep bow. "You are quite welcome, m'lady."

Behind her, Sophie could hear Lacie wailing, "She did NOT just curtsy to that guy!"

And she could hear Zeke yelling, "Mama! Sophie almost fell in the water!"

But all she really LISTENED to were the words of Mr. Messenger as he smiled down at her.

"You are a student of history, aren't you?" he said.

"I am. I make my own historical films — well, with my friends."

"And I imagine they are spectacular. How would you like to take a peek under these tarps here and see the chimney foundation and the floorboards of a house they've found?"

Sophie looked over at an area as big as their garage at home that was covered with a sheet of thick green plastic, and her heart started to pound.

"Oh, yes, sir, please!" Antoinette cried. She clasped the kind man's hands in hers and looked up with tears shining in her eyes. "I would give anything to know more about those brave men and women who came before me and suffered so much for this new land —"

"You better keep an eye on her, Rusty — she'll go off with anybody!"

Sophie turned to glare at Uncle Preston, but there wasn't even time to narrow her eyes. Daddy suddenly had her by the arm, pulling her hands away from Mr. Messenger.

"That's okay," Daddy said to him. "We're headed off for the gift shop. We have a lot of ground to cover today."

With that, he dragged Sophie away. She barely got a wave in to Mr. Messenger before Daddy was halfway into a lecture. Something about never being able to take her anywhere because she wasn't a team player.

Sophie didn't hear most of it. She let her eyes, and her ears, glaze over.

2

wouldn't have wanted to live in the seventeenth century because there were no malls, and Uncle Preston flipped through radio stations trying to get the Texas game, Sophie stared out at the drizzle and did what she did best. She imagined. *I can't be Antoinette AND be an archaeologist,* she thought. *But I can be LIKE Antoinette and Captain John Smith: I will be a pioneer for all that is more good than evil.*

Then she dreamed some more until she came up with the perfect name: *Dr. Demetria Diggerty.*

Of course, Sophie knew she would have to give Dr. Diggerty more than just a name, and to do that she needed quiet time in her room. So it really didn't bother her that almost as soon as they got back to the house late that afternoon, she heard Aunt Bailey and Lacie go off to the movies without inviting her. What DID bother her was that the minute the house was quiet, with Mama and Zeke off to the grocery store to buy stuff for supper and Uncle Preston dozing in front of football on TV, Daddy came immediately to Sophie's room.

Sophie curled WAY up on the purple rug in the library corner of her room. Daddy didn't waste any words. He didn't even sit down.

"Look," he said, pointing at her from his towering height, "I'm trying to understand you, Sophie. I've had the sessions with Dr. Peter, I got you the camera, and I'll let you keep it as long as you keep improving in school."

He paused, and since Sophie didn't know what she was supposed to say, she just shrugged.

"What does that mean?" Daddy said.

"It means I don't know what to say."

"You don't know what to say when I give you all that leeway and you still abuse it?"

Now Sophie REALLY didn't know what to say. She didn't even understand what he was talking about.

"I asked you to *stay* with the group and I *told* you why." Daddy was poking his finger toward her, one jab for each word that came out louder than the rest. "But could you *do* that? *No.* The *first* chance you got, you were *hanging* back with the guide, acting like one of your *pretend* characters. We don't *know* that man, *Sophie.* You don't go *grabbing* onto STRANGERS!"

Sophie plastered herself against the wall. She hadn't seen Daddy this mad since the day Zeke had "run away from home" to hide underneath the workbench in the garage. Sophie had found him and gotten him to pretend with her that they were like wounded soldiers coming home after a war so she could get him out. Only they got so wrapped up in the game, Sophie forgot to tell anybody where they were, and Mama was just calling the police when Lacie located them. Just like then, Daddy's face was now scarlet, and his eyes were in sharp points of blue. Sophie swallowed hard.

"Do you understand why I'm so upset with you?" Daddy said.

Sophie didn't, but she nodded anyway. He paused for a long time, and when she couldn't stand it any more, she said, "What's my punishment going to be?"

"You're already having it," he said. "I wouldn't let Bailey take you to the movies with Lacie."

It was all Sophie could do not to break into the biggest grin ever. She bit at her lip and gave him a solemn nod.

"I want you to sit in here tonight and think about what happens when you're not aware of your surroundings." Her father's voice was still stern, but at least he'd stopped poking his finger at her. "The whole purpose of giving you that camera was so you would limit your day-dreaming to filming."

Sophie opened her mouth to say, "If you would've just let me TAKE the camera WITH me" — but she decided against it. Daddy's face was returning to its natural color. It was better not to take any chances.

"Think about it," he said to her. "And for the rest of the weekend, I'd better see some improvement in your being a team player, or I WILL take that camera away."

When Daddy closed the door behind him on his way out, Sophie was sure that HER face was scarlet.

Dr. Demetria Diggerty wouldn't put up with treatment like that, she wanted to scream. *SHE knows more about palisades and trenching techniques and metal armor breastplates than ANYBODY, including HIM. Nobody makes her feel like SHE's a moron — because she isn't.*

Dr. Peter — that was Sophie's therapist, and the coolest one she was sure, even though she didn't know any other psychologists — had taught her that when she got mad at her father or anybody else that she should imagine Jesus, not Antoinette, and she was pretty sure that applied to Dr. Demetria Diggerty, too. The Jesus in her mind, with his kind eyes, could always make her calm down and not hurl books across the room, and eventually she knew what to do.

But right now, she really didn't want Jesus to see her with her fists clenched and her head about to explode. It seemed safer to imagine what Dr. Diggerty looked like . . .

She would have to have short hair, swept back so it didn't get in her way when she was digging up Jamestown treasure, but still romantic — maybe with some streaks in it or something. And her eyes — they would be brown and intelligent and able to see what she was going to find even before she found it. She was that in tune with the earth and all that it was hiding about the past.

The next morning Sophie wanted to call Fiona as soon as she got up so they could start planning their film — a documentary on excavating Jamestown. Then she remembered that Fiona and her family were at Club Med for the weekend, and Kitty and the rest of the Munfords were away visiting grandparents. Sophie would have settled for curling up by the fireplace in the family room all day and reading the book Mama had bought at the Jamestown gift shop to get more ideas — but at breakfast, Aunt Bailey announced that she was taking the "women" shopping. One glance at Daddy, and Sophie knew she'd better not protest.

While he and Uncle Preston and Zeke took off to shoot baskets at the gym, Sophie piled into their old Suburban with the other "women." Mama looked about as excited about it as Sophic did, and she barely spoke a syllable the whole way there.

Who can get a word in anyway? Sophie thought. *Aunt Bailey and Lacie never shut up!*

They didn't—not the whole time they were shopping. It was its WORST when they went to the lingerie department at Dillard's. Sophie remembered too late that Aunt Bailey had told Lacie they were going to buy her new bras, or Sophie would have faked diarrhea and begged Mom to take her to the ladies' room. By the time she realized what was happening, Aunt Bailey had already borrowed a tape measure from the sales clerk and was wrapping it around Lacie's chest.

"You have such a cute figure, Lacie," Aunt Bailey said as she gave the tape a professional snap. "I don't think the bras you're wearing are showing it off at all."

"I think the bras she's wearing are just fine," Mama said. Her elfin lips were tight. They reminded Sophie of the top of a drawstring bag.

"A good bra is definitely expensive," Aunt Bailey said. "But don't worry about the price, Lynda. I'm treating."

Lacie held her arms out for Aunt Bailey to reposition the tape measure under her breasts. Sophie wanted to go through the floor, but it didn't seem to be bothering Lacie at all.

"Aunt Bailey can afford it, Mama," Lacie said. "She and Uncle Preston are DINKS."

"What?" Mama said.

"Double Income No Kids," Lacie said.

"That's right," Aunt Bailey said. "So let me treat the girl to a nice foundation garment or two." She suddenly swept her eyes, bright blue in her colored contacts, over Sophie. "I would buy Sophie some, too, but I don't see any signs of development there at all. "

Sophie crossed her arms over her chest and felt her face going BEYOND scarlet.

"She's a late bloomer," Mama said. She put her arm around Sophie's shoulders.

"Still," Aunt Bailey said. She tilted her head, its hair gelled into a dozen auburn flips, and gave Sophie a thorough going-over with her eyes. "She could use a little padded bra. That would be cute."

"No!" Sophie said. "I'm not gonna pretend I have breasts when I don't!"

"Why not?" Lacie said. "You pretend everything else."

"Lacie, that's enough," Mama said. "You two do the bra thing. Sophie and I are going to look around."

"Mama babies her so much," Sophie heard Lacie say to Aunt Bailey as she and Mama moved away. Sophie didn't look back at them, but she was sure Aunt Bailey was nodding and rolling her eyes.

"I'm not a baby," Sophie said to Mama when they were safely in the pajama aisle. "I just don't need a bra."

"No, you don't," Mama said. The drawstring mouth was loosening up, but only a little.

"I don't even see what good breasts do until you have babies and stuff anyway."

Mama even smiled then, in that impish way she had that Sophie loved. "I'm happy to hear that. But I don't want you to feel left out, since Lacie is getting something."

"I'd rather have a trowel," Sophie said.

Mama's eyebrows went up as if she'd just made a discovery. "Ah, so that's what you're dreaming up now. You and the girls going to make the next Indiana Jones movie?"

Sophie shook her head firmly. "Better than Indiana Jones. We're going to be girl archaeologists and make amazing discoveries. That's why I need a trowel."

But they didn't have trowels in Dillard's, and since they were only going into stores Aunt Bailey wanted to go in, Mama suggested a couple of pretty little camisoles for Sophie to wear under her clothes, now that the weather was getting colder and she needed layers. "Since you don't have any body fat," Mama said.

Sophie tried on the camisoles, and she did have to admit they felt silky and good next to her skin, sort of grown-up. She was pretty sure Dr. Demetria Diggerty would wear something like that.

Later, when they were waiting for Aunt Bailey to decide between four different pairs of black boots, with Lacie's help, Mama put her arm around Sophie again and whispered to her that every girl developed at a different rate. That helped when, after purchasing three of the four pairs of boots, Aunt Bailey treated them to TCBY and went on about how gorgeous Lacie was becoming until Sophie was too nauseous to even eat her chocolate/vanilla swirl with Gummy Bears.

When Sunday came, Sophie stood on the front porch and made sure Daddy was REALLY going to take Aunt Bailey and Uncle Preston to the airport. Sophie had never been so happy to see somebody leave.

Monday morning on the bus, Sophie had no sooner pulled out her planning notebook to dream up some more details about Dr. Diggerty when the two girls in front of her turned around, up on their knees, to face her.

"Hey," one of them said.

Sophie knew both their names because they were in her class, although they had never really talked to her much until she had started riding the bus a few weeks before. The one in the Redskins sweatshirt was Harley Hunter. Her friend was Gillian Cooper, only everybody called her "Gill" with a hard "G" like in "girl."

Harley was sort of husky and she was always grinning, so that her cheeks came up and made her eyes almost disappear. Her sandy hair was cut short, and she gelled it so it would stand up.

It was hard to remember that Gill even HAD hair, because she wore a hat as often as she could get away with it. Today her reddish hair, which was as lanky as her long body, was tucked up into a green newsboy cap, the kind Daddy always said looked like an old-fashioned golfer's hat. It matched her green fleece jacket and her eyes.

"Hey," Sophie said back to them. And then she couldn't think what else to say. Gill and Harley were two of the four jock girls in her class, all into sports, and Sophie was always afraid they'd be like Lacie and start bugging her because she didn't play soccer or something.

"Me and her have been talking," Gill said, jabbing a thumb in Harley's direction, "and we decided you rock."

For a few seconds, Sophie could only stare. She finally found enough of her high-pitched little voice to say, "I rock? How come?"

"You and Fiona took DOWN the popular girls," Gill said. "You didn't let them run over you like they do everybody else."

Sophie knew they were talking about the Corn Pops as she and Fiona and Kitty — the Corn *Flakes* — referred to them in private. They were the pretty, smart, everybody-likes-me girls led by queen bee Julia Cummings. She had three worker bees — B.J. Freeman and Anne-Stuart Riggins and Willoughby Wiley. There had been a fourth one until Kitty had become a Corn Flake. She had almost had to, to protect herself against the Corn Pops. They weren't the sweetest box of cereal on the shelf.

Gill gave Sophie a friendly punch on the arm. "You even made the teachers see that those girls aren't all that, the way they always thought they were since, like, kindergarten."

Harley punched Sophie's other shoulder. "You rock," she said.

I like rocking, Sophie decided as she got off the bus. *I think Dr. Demetria Diggerty rocks, too, and people know it.*

Thinking of the good doctor, Sophie headed for the playground where Fiona and Kitty always waited for her before school, almost bursting open with what she knew Fiona would call "a scathingly brilliant idea." Fiona had the best vocabulary of any kid in sixth grade — or maybe even all of Great Marsh Elementary.

They were on the swings when she got there, and Sophie barely let them say hello before she was launching into details.

Fiona watched her carefully out of her wonderful gray eyes, one stream of golden-brown hair erupting from her knitted striped beanie cap and over the side of her face. Sophie always thought that made her best friend look exotic.

Kitty followed Sophie with her eyebrows knit together over her big blue eyes like she wasn't quite getting it. When Sophie was finishing up the details, Kitty played nervously with her ponytail of ringlets.

"Are we going to have to act all weird when we make this movie?" she said. "It sounds like it."

Fiona pulled her lips into their perfect heart shape. "It isn't being weird," she said. "It's being an actor."

"I don't know if I can do that, though." Kitty's voice curled up into a whine. "I'll get all nervous."

"When you're yourself," Sophie said, "it's never weird. Remember — that's our Corn Flakes motto."

Kitty pressed her lips together until her dimples punctured her cheeks. Kitty, Sophie knew, still wasn't sure about being a full-fledged Corn Flake.

The bell rang and they hurried into the building, Sophie and Fiona already puzzling over exactly what was going to happen in their movie.

"I think we should do an actual dig," Fiona said. "And we can make the movie about the stuff we find."

"I LOVE that!" Sophie said.

"She LOVES that," someone said behind her, in a high-pitched voice that mocked Sophie's.

"If she loves it," someone else said, "then it's got to be something WAY lame."

Sophie didn't even have to turn around to know it was the Corn Pops.

3

couldn't miss it, "or they wouldn't be talking like that."

Sophie glanced down the hall. She could see the BACK of Mr. Denton's balding head gleaming in the overhead lights as he stood outside the door of the Language Arts room. That would explain why Julia was taking a chance being rude.

Still, Sophie thought, *she should be careful.*
IF ANY of the Corn Pops are caught being
evil, they're toast.

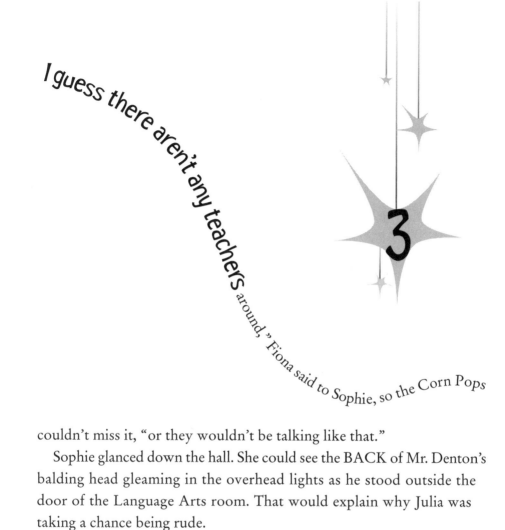

Beside her, Kitty whimpered and clung to Sophie's arm. Fiona rolled her eyes.

"Kitty, when are you going to figure out that they can't hurt you any-more?" she said.

Fiona looked straight at Julia, who tossed her thick, auburn hair and let it bounce back into place across the shoulders of her red polo dress. It matched the one B.J. was wearing, only hers was dark blue. B.J. tossing HER shiny short bob of butter-blonde didn't have quite the same effect as when Julia did it, but, then, SHE wasn't the Queen Bee.

"Don't be so sure about that," B.J. said.

But the third Pop, Anne-Stuart, nudged her with a bony elbow and said, "When did we ever hurt Kitty to begin with?"

Sophie took another quick look back at Mr. Denton. He was turning their way, and all three of the Corn Pops' faces spread into practiced smiles.

"Whatever," Julia said, and she swept off down the hall with Anne-Stuart and B.J. behind her, still beaming at Mr. Denton.

"Are you three behaving yourselves?" he said as they hurried past him into the room.

"Yes, sir!" Anne-Stuart said. And then she gave a juicy sniff. Sophie always thought Anne-Stuart must have the worst sinuses in York County.

Fiona led the Corn Flakes toward the room, and they all grinned at Mr. Denton.

"Everything okay?" he said.

"YES," Sophie said, and she squeezed Kitty's hand.

Mr. Denton nodded. "You let me know if it isn't."

"See?" Fiona said to Kitty as walked in. "You have absolutely nothing to worry about."

That was true, and Sophie knew it. HER only real worry was that she needed to improve by at least a point in each of her classes this week so she could keep on using her video camera. She was dying to try some of the old spellings of things she'd read about in her Jamestown book, like "meddows" and "blud" and "peece" — and her personal favorite, "dyinge," for "dying." But she decided this wasn't the time to have Mr. Denton counting off on her paper. She did manage to slip one of the new words she'd learned from the book — "vexations" — into one of her vocabulary word sentences, just to impress him.

At lunchtime that day, when Fiona, Kitty, and Sophie were settling in at their usual cafeteria table, Harley and Gill came up, zippered lunch bags in hand.

"Can we sit with you guys?" Gill said. She had taken off the green newsboy cap, and her hair was shoved back on one side with a barrette shaped like a soccer ball.

"Absolutely you can," Sophie said.

"Them, too?" Harley said.

She jerked her spiky head back at their two friends that Sophie knew were Nikki and Yvette, although she didn't know which was which because they were identical twins, with short blonder-than-blonde hair that they were always tucking behind their ears to keep it from falling into their faces.

"Y'all know Nikki and Yvette?" Sophie said to Kitty and Fiona.

"It's 'Vette," Gill informed them. "Like short for CORvette. They're very into cars."

"Can they talk?" Fiona said.

"Of course they can talk," Gill said.

"Just asking," Fiona said.

A conversation began about just how many cars the twins' dad had in his collection, but Sophie's attention wandered to the far end of the table, where a stocky girl with very dark chin-length hair and skin the color of pancake syrup was watching the Corn Flakes and the "jocks."

Maybe they could be the Wheaties, Sophie thought.

Then she grinned at the dark girl. "Hey, Maggie," she said. "Why don't you come down here and sit with us?"

"Because I don't want to be a Corn Flake," Maggie said.

As usual, every one of Maggie's words fell into the air like a bag of flour being dropped to the floor. Sophie sagged. That was the answer she always got, ever since she and Fiona had dumped Maggie a while back. Even though Sophie asked her to hang out with them about three times a week, Maggie always said the same thing. Mama had told Sophie that some people would hold a grudge forever.

Sophie felt a nudge in the back and turned to find a plastic container practically in her face.

"Want one?" Harley said.

"Her mom always starts baking Christmas cookies the day after Thanksgiving," Gill said. "Take one of the snowflakes. They, like, disappear in your mouth. "

"I like these surprise bar things better," Fiona said. She was currently splitting one open to share with Kitty, who already had several dabs of chocolate on her upper lip.

"Harley doesn't share these with just anybody," Gill said. "This is 'cause you guys rock."

The belonging-feeling that Sophie suddenly had inside her chest was almost enough to make her want to go out for basketball or something, just for the Wheaties Girls. She looked around the table at the six of them who surrounded her.

Who woulda thought just two months ago that I would have even ONE friend, much less this many? Sophie thought.

And even though they were all way different, everybody was getting along, which was the best part.

I betcha Dr. Peter would say this was like Jesus, she thought. *Sitting down at the table with all different people that nobody else understood.*

She would be seeing Dr. Peter the next day. She decided she'd have to tell him about this.

"Excuse me," somebody said in a sniffling voice.

"What do you want, Anne-Stuart?" Fiona said. She was never one for being more friendly to a Corn Pop than she had to be, even if the Pop was smiling like a packet of Sweet-and-Low the way Anne-Stuart was doing right now.

Anne-Stuart pulled her skinny self up to her tallest and gave her neck a nervous-looking jerk. It sent a ripple through the perfect sandy hair pulled back by a black suede headband, an exact match for her mini-skirt and boots. Sophie knew Aunt Bailey would have said that was NOT a good look for someone with legs that scrawny.

"I'm taking a survey," Anne-Stuart said. She tapped a pad of lavender lined paper with a perfectly sharpened pencil that didn't even have any teeth marks in it yet.

"What kind of survey?" Fiona said.

By now Kitty had her head buried behind Fiona's shoulder. Harley was straightening hers.

"I'm asking all the girls: who wears a bra and what size is it?"

"None of your business," Maggie said from the far end.

She shoved an uneaten banana into her lunch bag and got up and left.

Anne-Stuart appeared to be making a note on her pad, and then she looked expectantly at Gill.

"We all wear 'em," Gill said, pointing to the three Wheaties.

Anne-Stuart nodded and scribbled like she was taking down votes for the Presidential election. "What sizes?" she said.

"Medium," Gill said, jabbing a finger toward Harley. "The rest of us wear smalls."

There was a thick sniff from Anne-Stuart. "Then you all don't really wear bras or you would know that they don't come in small, medium, and large." She turned the pencil over impatiently and started to erase.

"Shows what you know," Gill said. "These are sports bras."

"Oh," Anne-Stuart said. She puckered her almost-invisible eyebrows in a frown and then looked at Fiona.

"I'm only telling you this because I know if you try to use it for something evil, you'll get kicked out of school," Fiona said. "I wear a thirty, double-A."

Sophie stared at her. She'd had no idea Fiona wore a bra. She suddenly felt like her own chest was shrinking.

"And you?" Anne-Stuart said, bulging her watery eyes at Kitty.

"Tell her, Kit," Fiona said, giving her a jab in the ribs Sophie could almost feel.

Kitty kept her gaze glued to the tabletop. "I wear a thirty-two, A," she said. Sophie could hardly hear her.

Anne-Stuart obviously did, because she pulled the pad into her chest and shook her head at Kitty. "You know that's not true," she said. "You can't possibly wear a bigger size bra than I do."

"What do you want her to do, pull off her sweater and show you the tag?" Fiona said.

"No!" Kitty said.

"No, I do not," Anne-Stuart said. "But I'm putting a question mark next to it."

Anne-Stuart made that notation with a flourish, and then she looked at Sophie. Her eyes were expectant, as if she had been saving the best for last.

"How about you, Sophie?" she said.

If I don't answer, Sophie thought, *Anne-Stuart will go back to the Corn Pops and tell them she had me scared or something. NO WAY!*

Still, she could feel her face burning as she adjusted her glasses on her nose and looked over the top of them at Anne-Stuart. "I prefer not to wear a bra," she said. "I wear a camisole."

Anne-Stuart gave the biggest snot-snort yet. "Doesn't have any breasts yet," she said as she wrote on her pad. Then she gave them her Nutra-Sweet smile, turned on the heel of her black suede boot, and pranced to the Corn Pops table, where Julia, B.J., and Willoughby were sitting on the edges of their seats as if Anne-Stuart were going to come back and announce the Academy Awards.

"They are just as heinous as they ever were," Fiona said. "I think we conducted ourselves like mature women."

Harley gave her a blank look. "Because I didn't get up and punch her out?" she said.

"Pretty much," Fiona said.

Sophie slid down in her seat and pulled open her turkey sandwich. Mama had put cranberry sauce on it, just the way she liked it, but she couldn't have eaten if she'd been starving to death.

Why did I get all embarrassed over that? she thought. *Stuff like body things never made me turn red before—*

At least until everybody on the planet started talking about the breasts I don't have!

"Hey, Soph."

Sophie looked up quickly at Fiona.

"We're over them," she said. She darted her eyes quickly at Kitty, who was cowering at Fiona's side.

"We are SO over them," Sophie said. She stretched so she could get closer to Kitty. "As a matter of fact, what was she talking about? I forget already."

"I'm thinking we should be concentrating on starting our movie after school," Fiona said.

Sophie gave her head a firm nod, the way she knew Dr. Demetria Diggerty would.

"The digging begins this afternoon—my backyard. Bring your trowels."

4

Diggerty as she gathered the white buckets and the trowels and headed for the site where her two eager assistants were waiting to begin.

"What are your names?" Dr. Diggerty said.

"Artifacta Allen," said the mysterious one with the wonderful gray eyes.

"Kitty Munford," said the other one.

"No," Sophie said. She tried to keep her voice patient. "What is your name going to be in the film?"

Kitty looked around blankly. "I don't see the camera."

"We have to plan first," Fiona said — LESS than patiently.

Sophie handed each of them one of Mama's small gardening shovels. She hadn't asked Mama if she could use them before she left with Zeke to set up for the bake sale Lacie's basketball team was having, but Sophie was sure it would be okay. After all, Mama had been excited about Jamestown treasure herself.

"Just be thinking of a name, Kitty," Sophie said. "For now, we'll just call you — "

"Kitty," Kitty said.

Sophie knelt down on the damp ground at the edge of the square she had drawn out in the dirt with a pointed stick in the back corner of the LaCroix's yard.

"According to the documental evidence I have obtained," Sophie — Dr. Demetria Diggerty — said, "this is a likely place to find artifacts."

"What's documental evidence?" Kitty said.

"You would already know that if you were an archaeologist," Fiona said.

"But I'm not!" Kitty said.

"You're supposed to pretend!"

"Oh," Kitty said.

Sophie patted her hand. "Maybe you should just listen at first, until you get the hang of it."

Kitty nodded glumly.

Sophie pushed her glasses up on her nose and went on. "Remember that we must scrape off only an eighth of an inch of dirt at a time and put it on the screens."

Sophie pointed a proud finger at the old pieces of screen she had placed over the openings of the white buckets.

"Why?" Kitty said.

Fiona gave a sigh that sounded as if it came from the pit of her stomach.

"So any pieces of artifacts will stay on the screen and the dirt will fall through," Sophie said.

Kitty craned her neck toward the buckets. "Those are going to be some pretty small articles."

"Artifacts!" Fiona practically screamed at her. Fiona's skin blushed toward the shade of a radish.

"I don't even think the dirt is going to go through holes that small," Kitty said.

Sophie had to admit she was probably right. "Okay," she said. "We won't use the screens. We'll just look at our dirt and if there's anything in it, we'll put it in this bucket, and we'll put the dirt in that bucket."

"Excellent plan, Doctor," Fiona said. "You amaze me with your expertise."

"Her what?" Kitty said.

Fiona sighed again. "Just pretend you know what I'm talking about, okay?"

They all went to work with their trowels, carefully scraping off soil with the sides of them, examining it closely for signs of armor or seventeenth century pottery, and dumping the dirt into the buckets.

After ten minutes, Dr. Demetria Diggerty's hand was starting to hurt, and Kitty was complaining that this was boring and that she was freezing. Even Artifacta Allen rocked back on her heels and said, "This is going to take forever, Soph—Doctor. I doubt that we're going to find any valuable evidence until we've dug down further."

"Yeah," Kitty said. "Don't you have any bigger shovels?"

That isn't the way they do it! Sophie wanted to say to them. But she knew if she did, Kitty would abandon the whole thing, and she and Fiona were determined to show Kitty that it was far better to be a Corn Flake than a Corn Pop.

She adjusted her Winnie-the-Pooh ball cap—the closest thing she could find to those hats the archaeologists at Jamestown were wearing—and nodded slowly.

"Agreed," she said. "Let's dig down two feet before we start sifting again."

"I would suggest three," Fiona said.

Kitty didn't say anything. She was already coming out of the garage dragging three shovels.

So they went to work again, talking as much like archaeologists as they could and hauling out huge shovelfuls of dirt and piling it against the fence. It turned out to be a lot more fun than scraping off tiny bits at a time, and even when it started to drizzle and Sophie had to wipe off her glasses every few minutes, they kept on; "spirits high!" as Fiona put it. In spite of her whining that it was time to get the camera out, Kitty got into the project, too.

"I wanna be the first one to have my shovel hit the buried treasure chest," she said.

Both Fiona and Sophie stopped and stared at her.

"It's not that kind of treasure we're looking for," Sophie said.

"Then what is it?" Kitty said.

"Don't you remember, Madam Munford?" Fiona said between her teeth. "We are searching for small things that will help us understand the way the people before us lived."

Kitty poked her shovel back into the now very wet dirt. "I think they left a treasure chest," she said, and kept digging.

Dr. Demetria Diggerty smiled to herself. Perhaps she didn't have the brightest assistant in the field, but at least she was enthusiastic. By the time the camera crew arrived to film their progress, Madam Munford would be as professional as she and Artifacta were. She lifted her head from her digging to tell them both how much she appreciated their hard-working attitudes — and found herself looking right up into Daddy's scarlet face.

"Sophie — what in the world are you THINKING!"

Kitty whimpered, dropped her shovel with a splash into the hole, and took off toward the house, crying, "I have to call my mom. I have to go home!"

Fiona, on the other hand, leaned on her shovel and wafted an arm over their handiwork. "This is an archaeological dig," she said.

"No," Daddy said. "This is a mess. Sophie — you know what it took for your mother and me to put this yard in last summer — and here you are digging it up! What were you thinking?"

"I was thinking we would find some artifacts," Sophie said.

"And I'M thinking you're going to find the sprinkler system and chop a hole in a line!"

"We would know a sprinkler pipe wasn't an artifact, Mr. LaCroix," Fiona said. "We're professionals."

"Fiona," Daddy said, with his eyes still boring into Sophie, "go call your Boppa to come pick you up."

"Right now?" Fiona said.

"Go, Artifacta," Sophie said. "I will contact you later."

"Don't count on it, 'Artifacta'," Daddy said as Fiona reluctantly put down her shovel and trudged toward the house. "Sophie is going to be out of the loop for a while."

Sophie could feel Dr. Demetria Diggerty fighting to take over, yearning to turn and call to her colleague, "Don't worry. I will find a way. We will not be kept from our duty to history" — but she strained to stay focused on Daddy. It sounded like she was in enough trouble already.

"Artifacta?" Daddy said. "Never mind." He ran a hand over his hair as he looked down at the hole they'd been so proud of a few minutes before. His eyes were still blazing.

"I can't believe you did this," he said. "Is all that therapy doing any good at all?"

"Yes," Sophie said. "I'm making good grades. I have friends now — "

38

"You have friends, all right. Friends that aren't any more responsible than you are." Daddy snatched Sophie's shovel from her and picked up the other two with one hand. She could see the muscles in his jaw going into spasms. He looked over at the pile of dirt that had now turned to mud against the fence, and groaned.

"All right, here's the deal," he said. "It looks to me like you need some time apart from your 'friends' so you can think about your responsibilities. One week — "

A whole WEEK? Just for a hole? "No phone, no e-mail, no TV, no camera."

"Can't I just fill in the hole and let that be my punishment?" Sophie said.

"Go to your room, Sophie," Daddy said, "before I say something we'll both regret."

Dr. Demetria Diggerty stormed to her living quarters, her dignity dashed and her project in ruins. But as she slammed her door behind her and hurled herself across her cot, she swore with her fists doubled that even the evil Enemy of History, Master LaCroix, would not stand in her way.

But that didn't help much. Sophie sat up on her bed and hugged a purple pillow against her chest.

Jesus, she thought. *I'm supposed to imagine Jesus when I get mad — not Dr. Diggerty.*

She closed her eyes and tried to picture the kind man who always seemed to understand. She could almost see him — but not quite. His edges were fuzzy this time.

Sophie squeezed her eyes shut tighter and tried some more. *I know you love me, Jesus. There aren't any ifs anymore. I know you're there —*

But she couldn't quite see his face in her mind. It was a good thing, she decided, that the next day was a Dr. Peter day.

Daddy told her that night, when he came in to get the camera, that he couldn't keep her from being with her friends at school, but he "advised her" to spend any of her free time there working on her studies and "getting serious". She didn't remind him that there wasn't much point in getting good grades if she didn't get to have her camera anyway. She decided it would be better to discuss that with Dr. Peter.

So all day long she suffered through Kitty's tearful looks and Fiona's notes asking her why she didn't stage a mutiny on her father, which was what SHE would do. Finally, school was over and Mama picked her up to take her to Hampton for her appointment.

At first they rode in stiff silence, as if the air between them had been spray-starched. All Sophie could think about was that if Mama was going to go along with this heinous punishment, she couldn't confide in her. She didn't know WHAT Mama was thinking.

"Do you want to talk about it?" Mama said finally.

"No, thank you," Sophie said.

But she did squirm in her seat belt and say, "I'm sorry if it upset you that I dug a hole in the yard. I didn't think you would mind."

"We don't always know what people would and wouldn't mind about what belongs to them," Mama said. "That's why we ask first."

But you weren't there! Sophie wanted to say. *You were off doing something for Lacie. Like usual.*

Sophie even turned to her to maybe say SOME of that, but Mama looked as if she were already thinking about something else. Something that had nothing to do with her.

The minute Mama pulled up to the clinic, Sophie was out of the Suburban and inside Dr. Peter's office. As always, he was waiting for her at the front counter with a "Sophie-Lophie-Loodle! Good to see you!"

"We need to talk," she said.

"Of course," he said. His face grew serious and his blue eyes stopped twinkling behind his glasses. "That's what I'm here for."

Sophie climbed up onto the window seat in Dr. Peter's office and grabbed one of the face pillows to crunch against her. She could feel a stuffed nose pressing into her chest, and she plucked angrily at an ear that poked out the side.

"Okay, Loodle," Dr. Peter said when he was settled at the other end of the seat. "Give me the goods."

She did, pouring out everything, good and evil. Aunt Bailey and Uncle Preston. Jamestown. Dr. Demetria Diggerty. Bra shopping. And, of course, the hideous groundation punishment.

"And you know what's the absolute worst?" she said, when she had come to the end.

Dr. Peter shook his head of short, curly, reddish brown hair. He was looking at her soberly.

"I tried to imagine Jesus so I could ask for help — and then I was gonna wait for it, like you taught me — only it didn't work."

"You didn't get the help yet?"

"No! I couldn't even imagine his face!" Sophie swallowed hard. "I needed to see his eyes in my mind."

"And it upset you that you couldn't."

Sophie nodded. "Are you sure he's really always there? He doesn't get busy with somebody else's stuff?"

"I'm absolutely sure. That's the cool thing about Jesus: with him, it's always all about you and him, just like it's all about me and him, and all about whoever and him."

"Then where is he?" Sophie said.

Dr. Peter pressed his hand against his chest. "He's in there. We know that for sure, because you always fill up your space with the things that God loves."

"Then I guess I had some No-God space last night," Sophie said.

The serious face broke into a crinkly road map of smiling lines. "I like that, Loodle. There can be only two types of space within a person, God and No-God. Where we want to stay is our choice."

"I want to stay in God-space! Only it's hard when I'm mad."

"Understood," Dr. Peter said. "But you can stay in God-space if you know more about Jesus — what he was like on earth and still is in Spirit. Hey — " His eyes sparked to life again. "You want to do a little archaeology into Jesus's childhood?"

Sophie squinted at him through her glasses. "Wouldn't we have to go to Nazareth to do that?"

"Nope — although wouldn't we have a blast?"

Sophie had to agree that they would. In fact, she had to work hard for a minute to keep Dr. Demetria Diggerty from taking completely over and planning the trip.

"No, our best site for digging," Dr. Peter went on, "is in the Gospel of Luke. I'm going to write down some Bible verses for you to read and picture in your mind. It sounds like you're going to have plenty of time for that this week."

Sophie scowled. "I sure hope this works," she said. "'Cause I'm tired of getting mad all the time."

Dr. Peter let a silence fall, though it wasn't a starched-up one like she had sat through with Mama in the car. While he was writing on a piece of paper with a purple Sharpie, Sophie sighed back into the cushions and let her thoughts settle down.

"Tell me something, Loodle," Dr. Peter said finally. His voice was soft. "What do you want most in the world right now, right this very second?"

Sophie didn't even have to think about it. "I want my father to stand up for me, just once," she said. "Instead of always saying everything that happens is my fault and telling me what I should have done different."

Dr. Peter nodded as he handed her the paper. "It's time to dig in with God, then, Loodle. I think this is going to help you meet the challenge."

Dig in. Meet a challenge.

Now THOSE sounded like words for Dr. Demetria Diggerty. Sophie took the paper and gave Dr. Peter a promise nod.

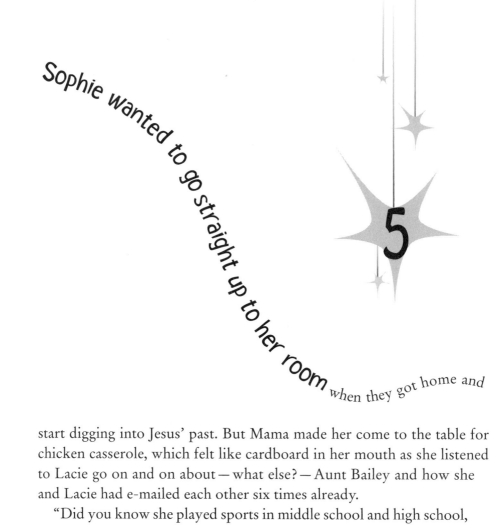

Sophie wanted to go straight up to her room when they got home and

5

start digging into Jesus' past. But Mama made her come to the table for chicken casserole, which felt like cardboard in her mouth as she listened to Lacie go on and on about — what else? — Aunt Bailey and how she and Lacie had e-mailed each other six times already.

"Did you know she played sports in middle school and high school, too, just like me?" Lacie said.

"Really?" Daddy said. "My brother never mentioned that to me."

"She did," Lacie said. "And she was good — especially in basketball — "

"Well, isn't that special?" Mama pushed back her chair and picked up the still-almost-full muffin basket. "We need more bread," she said, and she disappeared into the kitchen.

"I didn't even get one yet!" Zeke wailed.

Sophie stuck hers on his plate.

"Is Mom still mad at you because Aunt Bailey and Uncle Preston came here for Thanksgiving instead of us going to see Grandpa?" Lacie said to Daddy.

"Where did you get that idea?" Daddy said. He touched Lacie lightly on the nose and added, "Pass the salad dressing, would you?"

"Oh, come on," Lacie said. "She's been all tense since before they even came. All snappin' at me." Lacie lowered her voice as if she and Daddy were in on some kind of conspiracy. "I think she's a little jealous because Aunt Bailey and I got along so good."

Oh, for Pete's sake! Sophie thought. *Mama isn't some Corn Pop. Who CARES about Aunt Bailey?*

SHE certainly didn't. What she cared about was getting up to her room so she could start digging. She stuffed a couple of forks of asparagus into her mouth, chewed furiously and said, with her cheeks still packed, "I'm full. Can I be excused?"

Daddy nodded absently. He looked like what Lacie was saying was the most fascinating thing since the sports page.

Up in her room, Sophie pulled her Bible off the shelf and then settled herself precisely on her bed. This was going to be like using documental evidence, so she carefully arranged a sharpened pencil, with only a few teeth marks in it, her ideas notebook turned to a fresh page and, after some thought, her magnifying glass, just in case she needed to look VERY closely.

Then, with the anticipation of a new discovery coursing through her veins, Dr. Demetria Diggerty turned each page as if it were a fine piece of onion skin, until she reached the Gospel of Luke, chapter 2, verse 41. She held her breath —

Sophie stopped, breath still sucked in. Maybe she shouldn't dig as Dr. Diggerty.

If it was really going to help with the Daddy problem, she should probably do this as Sophie.

Still, she reached up on the headboard for her cap and set it in archaeological position on her head before she began to read.

It was the story about Jesus at age twelve going with his parents to Jerusalem for the Feast of the Passover. Sophie had heard the story before — probably about a bajillion times in Sunday school — but this time she tried to picture it as she read.

She could see Jesus finding the teachers in their long beards and fancy robes, sitting around on the stone floors of the magnificent temple. Jesus hanging out with them instead of going out partying with everyone else. And asking questions that echoed through the halls, impressing the sandals off of all the learned men.

She paused for a long time over the line, *Everyone who heard him was amazed at his understanding and his answers.*

"That's what I'M talkin' about," Sophie whispered.

She dug back in and read more and imagined Mary and Joseph bursting into the temple all scarlet-faced and chewing Jesus out because he had worried them sick. She could almost hear Mary saying that they had been looking all over for him — only it sounded more like Daddy's voice in her mind. Jesus' voice was clear and strong as he asked them why they were even worried about him when they should have known he'd be in his Father's house.

And then she got to the line that left no space for anything else: *But they did not understand what he was saying to them.*

Sophie closed the Bible and hugged it to her chest, her eyes closed so the picture of a frustrated twelve-year-old Jesus wouldn't go away. She imagined it for a long time — his confusion that they didn't know who he really was, the stirrings of anger he must have felt because they were mad at him for doing something that was only wrong to THEM. Again and again she could almost see his face as his parents looked at him, shaking their heads. *They did not understand what he was saying to them.*

"Wow," Sophie whispered. "I think I know exactly how you felt."

There was a tap on the door, and there was no time for Sophie to grab for her backpack and get out her homework before it opened and Mama came in. Sophie knew her face was as give-away guilty as Zeke's was whenever Mama caught him spitting mouthfuls of broccoli into his napkin.

"I'm starting my homework," Sophie said.

Mama cocked her head as she sat down on the end of Sophie's bed. "Did you think I was going to yell at you or something?"

"I was doing something else besides homework — well, SCHOOL homework."

"Honey," Mama said, "I would never scold you for reading the Bible! Give me a big ol' break!"

Sophie nodded and hoped Mama wasn't reading her mind. She was still thinking, *They did not understand . . .*

"I've come to make you an offer," Mama said. "I've talked this over with your father and he has given his okay IF you still get your schoolwork done."

"He's going to let me fill in the hole instead of being grounded!" Sophie said.

Mama just blinked. "No," she said. "He's already filled in the hole. And he wasn't happy about it."

"Oh," Sophie said. *No telling how much valuable physical evidence he covered back up.*

"Here is the deal," Mama said. "If you want to pursue your archaeology, you can start by digging in the attic while you're grounded. You know Uncle Preston brought that big trunk with him from Great-Grandma LaCroix's estate, and I haven't even opened it yet." Her eyebrows twitched. "He and Aunt Bailey said they don't want any of that 'old junk,' and I don't have time to go through it right now, so why don't you have a go at it? Maybe you could make me a detailed list of the contents. How would that be?"

"That would be incredible!" Sophie said.

"Just do it AFTER your homework is done. Maybe you shouldn't even think about doing it until this weekend. I just wanted to tell you now so you'll have something to look forward to."

Sophie threw her arms around Mama's neck — even though she wasn't sure that was something Dr. Demetria Diggerty would do.

"You are the best mom," she said.

"It's nice to hear that Tinker Bell laugh again, Dream Girl," Mama said.

When she was gone, Sophie sank back into her pillows and gazed up at her ceiling, dotted with fluorescent stars. She didn't really see them, though. She saw herself in the attic, an important-looking clipboard on her arm, peering through a magnifying glass at a piece of china so thin and old it had to go back as far as — maybe the 1950's or something . . .

And then she imagined the kind eyes of Jesus, and she decided she was back in God-space.

But it was hard to stay there for the whole next three days. Mama had been right that there would be no time to go into the attic until the weekend. In the meantime, although she worked hard to keep up with her homework, it was hard without Fiona to encourage her on the phone, or Kitty to keep her spirits up with the cheesy jokes she told her on the phone when she WASN'T grounded.

Besides, being home ALL the time meant that the things that drove her nuts were constantly all around her.

Lacie was "tearing it up" in basketball, as Daddy put it. When she was chosen captain of the team, Daddy brought home a cake with a miniature basketball hoop actually standing up on it. Zeke thought that was the coolest thing ever. Sophie felt shoved out.

Zeke, of course, was adorable, and she loved reading to him and playing games with him and his little plastic cars. But the day he dismantled the coffee maker, she was flabbergasted that HE didn't get grounded. He got a thirty-minute time-out, and Daddy explained to him how he could have hurt himself with the electricity—blah, blah, blah—but there was nowhere near the upheaval that had occurred when she dug one little hole in the backyard. She didn't want to resent her little brother, but she didn't feel as much like playing with him after that.

It was even hard with Mama. It wasn't that she was getting all "yelly" as Zeke would call it. In fact, she just kept being quieter and quieter, and once Sophie thought she heard her crying in the night when she got up to go to the bathroom. Back in bed, Sophie got Jesus in her mind and begged him to fix whatever was wrong with her mom.

It felt so much better to be in God-space for those few moments that Sophie decided to try harder to stay there. When Fiona and Kitty complained during lunch the next day about Sophie's groundation, Sophie told them the story about Jesus, and how she could relate to that because, like his parents, hers didn't understand her purpose either.

"Huh," Fiona said. "When it comes to LACIE'S purpose, your father is all over it."

That was true, and it sent Sophie scurrying to Dr. Diggerty, presenting an antique basketball hoop that she had pulled out of the rubble to the evil Master LaCroix, Enemy of History.

"Of what use is a rusty old piece of sports equipment?" he said to her. "I can buy hundreds of new ones. I see no further need for your services." Dr. Diggerty did not even lower her head. She knew he simply did not understand. She would fight for her career. She would fight to look though the lenses of the past ...

She felt a hard nudge in her ribs, and she jerked her head around. Harley was poking her. "She wants to say somethin' to ya," she said.

Sophie looked across the table at Maggie. Her face was set like cement.

"Maggie!" Sophie said. "You're sitting with us!"

"I'm only here to tell you something important." Maggie said.

"So dish," Fiona said. She leaned in on her elbow, chin in hand.

Maggie slanted her eyes at the Wheaties and the Corn Flakes, and then she pointed her eyes at Sophie. "There's a rumor going around about you."

"Let me guess who's spreading it," Fiona said. She glared past Maggie at the Corn Pops, who currently had their heads all bent over something on their table.

"That's right," Maggie said.

"I bet it's bad if they're spreading it," Kitty said. "No, I KNOW it's bad!"

"You know what?" Sophie said to Maggie. "I don't want to hear it."

Maggie gave her an open-eyed look. "You don't?"

"Nope. If it's a rumor, then it isn't true, so what do I care?"

"Sophie's right," Fiona said. She folded her arms across her chest. "It stops here."

"That's fine with me," Maggie said. She shoved her chair back and slung her lunch bag strap over her shoulder. "I just thought you'd want to know."

"Thanks," Sophie said.

"But no thanks," Fiona said.

Sophie felt a pang as Maggie trudged heavily away. Maybe if she had listened to what Maggie had to say, she would have stayed and they could have made things up to her —

But Harley banged her on the back and told her she rocked, and Sophie decided maybe that was just as good. Meanwhile, Kitty was gazing, wide-eyed, at Fiona.

"What?" Fiona said. "Do I have a booger hanging out of my nose or something?"

"You stood up for Sophie," Kitty said.

"Of course I did. We're Corn Flakes. We do that for each other."

"Oh," Kitty said.

That was Friday, the last school day before Sophie's grounding period was over.

"I'm gonna be so glad when Monday comes," Fiona told her as they were cramming their books into their lockers after school. "If we don't start playing again, I think I'm going to go into cardiac arrest."

Sophie knew that had something to do with dying, which didn't cheer her up much. "We only get to play if I improve at least a point in everything on my progress report Monday."

"You're going to, so quit stressing out. We need to be thinking about WHAT we're going to play — "

But Sophie suddenly had it. She had just emptied her backpack into her locker — because there was no homework over the weekend. That meant she could devote all her time to the excavation of the attic. What if —

"We could all three of us do our archaeology in my attic!" Sophie said. "This could be so cool — and my mother already said it was okay so we don't have to worry about my father yelling at us — well, me."

"Fabulous," Fiona said. Her eyes took on her deep, intrigued look. "You could develop a plan over the weekend so we can start Monday — "

"No — Tuesday. I have to wait 'til my dad gets home Monday to get off groundation."

"Okay — Tuesday. I'm going to work on Boppa for some actual hard hats like the archaeologists wear. He'll want to get out of the house anyway. We have a new nanny for Rory and Isabella, and she has so many rules, she's even starting to tell Boppa what to do!"

Boppa was Fiona's grandfather, who was like a mom and a dad to Fiona and her little brother and sister because her parents were WAY busy people and weren't around much. Sophie was sure Fiona would show up with something close to real-thing hats. Boppa didn't say no to her very often.

So Sophie went home that day with a lighter heart, and she started in on the attic right away, ball cap on backwards and notebook in hand. It wasn't an actual clipboard, but a pencil tucked behind her ear made her feel more professional.

Grandma Too was the name Lacie had given her as a little kid when she realized she had a Grandma, their father's mom, and HER mother was another Grandma, Too.

Once Sophie opened Grandma Too's trunk, the rest of the world ceased to exist. Inside were treasures like she never would have found in the backyard, she was sure, and her disappointment at not being able to use the trenching technique slowly faded.

There was a pair of Grandma Too's underwear, paper-thin and yellowed and as big as the shorts Lacie wore to play basketball in. The tag pinned to them with a rusty safety pin said she had worn them on her wedding day, in 1939.

"Very significant," Sophie said, and jotted that down in her notebook.

There were dried flowers, now in confetti flakes, from Too's bridal bouquet, and a gavel from when she was president of the

Ladies' Auxiliary. Sophie wasn't sure what that was, but it was engraved in the brass plate which she examined with her magnifying glass, so it must be historically important.

"This is the best," she murmured to herself. "The best, the best, the best."

She spent all of Friday evening going through the trunk, and she was up first thing Saturday, even before Zeke, and got back at it again. There was much work to be done.

But Dr. Demetria Diggerty was no stranger to hard work and long hours. These precious treasures had been hidden away for far too long, by those misers of historical knowledge, Preston and Bailey McEvil. "I will dig until I drop," Dr. Diggerty said. "I will not stop until I have discovered everything about the life of this amazing woman of another time and place —"

"Daddy, do you hear her talking to herself?"

Sophie jumped and looked around. Was somebody else in the attic with her? Like Lacie?

It took Sophie a minute to realize that Lacie's voice, and then Daddy's, were coming through the floor. Of course. This part of the attic was right above Lacie's room.

Sophie — Dr. Diggerty — tried to return to her work, but it was as if she were being pulled by the ear to listen to them.

"I hear her," Daddy said. "But I think that's going to stop soon. She's starting to change."

"Right," Lacie said.

"And I think it's because of you, Lace."

"Are you kidding? Daddy, she won't listen to a thing I say."

Sophie heard the chair creak, and she knew Daddy was sitting down on the corner of it.

"You might not think she's listening, but she's watching you," Daddy said. "That's one of the reasons I grounded her, so she'd be around you more often. You're a good role model for her."

"Thanks, " Lacie said.

You have to be KIDDING! Sophie thought.

"You're always my go-to guy," Daddy said. "I know I can count on you."

As the chair creaked again and Lacie's door opened and closed, Sophie put her face into the pile of linens she'd pulled out of Grandma Too's trunk and decided this must be what it felt like to be an orphan.

I really, really know how you felt, Jesus, she thought with her eyes squeezed tight. Because now I know how MUCH my father doesn't understand.

6

When she couldn't be in the attic — like when they went to church and when Daddy took them all out to the Crab Cake House — she tried to imagine Jesus and how HE felt when HIS father didn't get HIM, either. All of that kept her from remembering what Daddy had said — about Lacie being a role model for her — and from worrying about whether she was going to improve on her progress report. She still didn't know what "cardiac arrest" was, but she was sure that she, like Fiona, was going to have it if she didn't get to start making films with the Corn Flakes again.

Monday, when Sophie saw the last grade of the last class, she decided that Jesus had been listening.

"What's the verdict?" Fiona whispered to her while their math and science teacher, Mrs. Utley, was passing out the rest of the progress reports.

Sophie gave her a slow smile. "Drum roll, please," she said.

Fiona nodded at Kitty, who giggled and rapped her hands several times on her desktop.

"Language Arts — up by three points."

"And?"

"Social Studies — up by FIVE points. That's because I did extra credit after I went to Jamestown . . ."

"Go ON, already!"

"Computers — up by one and a half points. Same with health."

"Whew — close one."

"Math — up by three points."

Kitty and Fiona didn't say anything this time. They seemed to be holding the same breath as they watched Sophie's lips.

"And science — up by one half of a point."

"No!" the Corn Flakes said together.

"You're right. I'm kidding," said Sophie. "Up by one point. One wonderful point!"

The three of them started to shout a collective "Yes!", but that drew a wiggle from one of Mrs. Utley's soft chins, so they settled for their secret pinkie handshake, done in clandestine fashion between the desks.

From across the room, Sophie caught Maggie watching them, and for a second Sophie thought she looked a little wishful. But as soon as her eyes met Maggie's, she busied herself with packing up her backpack. That was still a thing that had to be fixed, Sophie thought. But right now —

Right now it was time to celebrate. Well, almost. She still had to wait until Daddy got home from work, and when he didn't arrive until almost 6:30, she was convinced he was stalling on purpose.

By the time he came in the back door, she was pacing a path in the kitchen floor. The progress report was in his hand before Zeke could crawl up his leg or Lacie could get to him with her new free-throw average. They didn't even get to the kitchen.

"Don't worry—it's good," Sophie said as she watched Daddy's eyes sweep the page.

"You barely scraped by with getting the one-point improvement in a couple of subjects," he said. "But you met the requirements. I guess I have to give that camera back to you."

"And I'm off groundation, right?" Sophie said.

Daddy took his time putting his briefcase down and peeling off his jacket. He sure looked to Sophie as if he wanted to say no.

At last he sat down on a stool at the snack bar, so that at least he wasn't looking at her from his towering height. "Do you think you've learned something from being grounded?" he said.

"Yes," Sophie said.

"What?"

"That I shouldn't mess with other people's stuff—like their lawn—without asking first."

"That's it?"

Sophie blinked. "Is there supposed to be more?"

"Seems like it to me," Daddy said.

Actually, there WAS more in Sophie's mind, but she wasn't sure Daddy would want to hear it. She closed her eyes and tried to imagine Jesus, explaining HIS purpose to HIS parents. Maybe there was a way . . .

Passing up *I learned that you really do want me to be a clone of Lacie,* Sophie took a deep breath and said, "I learned that you want me to be a team player and do everything the way everybody else in the family does it."

Daddy started to nod, but then he didn't. His black eyebrows bunched together over his nose. "Anything else?"

"That's what I learned from YOU," she said.

Daddy leaned forward, like he was suddenly very interested. "So you learned some things from somebody else through all this?" he said.

Sophie almost nodded. She almost told him about the Jesus-story Dr. Peter had given her. She almost did. Until she remembered that conversation she'd heard through the attic floor.

He's thinking I learned something from Lacie, she thought. *No way. That is just — that's heinous!*

Daddy was still looking at her, his blue eyes waiting.

"I learned from Mama," she said, "that you don't have to dig holes in other people's property to be an archaeologist. I'm having great success in the attic."

It was as if someone had ripped a mask off of Daddy and left him with a totally different face. He sat back on the stool and rubbed his palms up and down his thighs. Sophie waited, holding her breath.

"Okay. You're free," he said, "but just — just think before you do things from now on, all right?"

Think like Lacie, you mean! Sophie wanted to cry out at him. But there was still one more question she wanted to ask, and she couldn't do anything to jeopardize the answer being YES.

"So is it okay if Kitty and Fiona come over and film in the attic with me tomorrow after school?" she said.

"Tomorrow is a Dr. Peter day," Mama said from behind them.

Sophie didn't know when she had slipped in. She was carrying a box with various Christmas decorations poking out the top.

"But I don't see why they can't come Wednesday," Mama said. "I'll have all the Christmas stuff out of the attic by then so I won't be in your way."

"We definitely wouldn't want to get in your way," Daddy said to Sophie.

"Hello!" Mama said.

Sophie looked quickly at her. The drawstring mouth was pulled so tight, she wasn't sure how Mama had gotten even that much out.

"Sorry — just messing around," Daddy said. He took the box from Mama. "Where do you want this?"

She jerked her curls toward the kitchen table.

"Sure, bring in the Dream Team," Daddy said over his shoulder to Sophie. "Just don't — "

"I know," Sophie said. "I'll be aware of my surroundings and I won't lose touch with the real world and I'll be a team player and I won't think everything is always all about me. Can I go to my room now?"

"Absolutely," Mama said.

As she made for the stairs, Sophie heard Daddy say, "What was that all about?"

She didn't hear what Mama said. She wasn't sure she wanted to.

It was still disappointing that Daddy was probably never going to stand behind her the way she wanted him to. But the next day at lunch as she looked at the happy cluster of girls at her table — Harley and Gill and Vette and Nikki and Kitty and Fiona, she decided she had plenty of other people to do that, and she felt her wisp of a smile forming.

It got bigger when Maggie plunked herself down across from her.

"You're here!" Sophie said.

"I just have a question for you," she said.

"Yes, you can still be a Corn Flake girl — anytime you want."

Maggie rolled her eyes. "You can give that up," she said. "It's a different question."

"So stop loitering around it and ask it," Fiona said.

"Only Sophie can answer it," Maggie said, every word heavy.

"Which she can only do if you ASK IT!" Fiona said.

Maggie ignored her. Her dark eyes were on Sophie. "Is it true that you're going to a psychiatrist?"

Sophie's tongue turned to stone right in her mouth. That was some-thing Kitty and Fiona already knew, and it was no big deal to them. But Harley and Gill and the twins didn't know about it. What were they going to think?

Sophie could feel her cheeks burning, and it was all she could do not to lower her head and pull her long hair over her face. But she didn't know why, not really. It had always been so easy to just be honest about things. Now she wasn't sure she could even get her tongue moving.

"That is SO nobody's business but Sophie's!" Fiona said.

"YOU know, though, don't you?" Maggie said to her.

"Only because she wanted to tell me — not because I plopped myself in the middle of her business and asked her!"

Gill put her mouth close to Sophie's ear. "Harley wants to know if you want her to kick Maggie's tail."

"No!" Sophie said. It was suddenly enough that they were stick-ing up for her. She straightened her shoulders. "I don't go to a psy-chiatrist," she said.

"See!" Gill said.

"I go to a child psychologist. He helps me figure things out so I can get better grades and have friends and understand about God."

"Oh," Maggie said. The expression on her face didn't change from its set-in-concrete stare. "So are you crazy or not?"

"No, she's not crazy!" Fiona said. "Does she ACT like she's crazy?"

Maggie shrugged. "Sometimes. When she's all pretending and stuff — it's like it's real to her."

"And this is a problem because?" Fiona said.

Maggie gave a final shrug and got up. "I was just asking," she said.

She lumbered off toward the trashcans.

"Thanks, y'all," Sophie said.

"Of course," Fiona said. And then she switched the subject to what everybody was asking for for Christmas.

Sophie couldn't wait to get settled in on the window seat that afternoon to tell Dr. Peter what she'd learned from the Bible verses and how it was working. She didn't even have to hug a face pillow while she was talking.

But to her surprise, he picked one up and toyed with its fuzzy eyebrows before he said, "So did you read the rest of it, Loodle?"

"There was more?"

"I love what you got out of that part." Dr. Peter wrinkled his nose so his glasses scooted up. "But what do you say we dig a little deeper, together? I have a surprise for you."

Sophie could feel her smile spreading practically to her ear lobes as Dr. Peter reached behind him and pulled out two helmets. They looked just like what explorers wore in those old movies about going on safaris and stuff. She had watched the animated version of *Tarzan* with Zeke enough times to recognize them immediately.

"Are these for us?" she said. She could hear her voice going up into its high-pitched squeal.

"A helmet for each of us," Dr. Peter said. He handed Sophie one and perched the other on top of his gel-stiff curls. "Because you never know what kind of jungle we might get into."

Sophie tucked her hair up into hers and although it came down to the tip of her nose and she had to tilt her head to see, she felt more like Dr. Demetria Diggerty than ever. But she concentrated on staying in Sophie-Land.

"All right, fellow explorer." Dr. Peter pulled out a Bible and a magnifying glass out of a daypack on the floor. "Just in case," he said. "Now, Luke 2, verse 51."

"I'll dig for it," Sophie said. She ruffled through the pages and located their excavation site. But she handed it back to Dr. Peter for the actual reading, so she could close her eyes and imagine.

"'Then he went down to Nazareth with them,'" Dr. Peter read. "'Them' would be his parents."

"I can see them," Sophie said. She nodded, eyes still closed. "Dig on."

"'Then he went down to Nazareth with them, and was obedient to them. But his mother treasured all these things in her heart. And Jesus grew in wisdom and stature, and in favor with God and men.'"

"What about his father?" Sophie said.

"It doesn't say anything about his father," Dr. Peter said.

"Okay. Go on."

"That's it."

Sophie opened her eyes. "But what happens after that?"

"The next time we see Jesus is when he's about thirty and he gets baptized by John the Baptist."

"Oh." Sophie could feel her eyebrows twisting. "So he didn't ever make his parents understand? He just had to find other people who did? And he didn't find them until he was THIRTY?"

Dr. Peter pulled out the magnifying glass and applied it to the page, brow furrowed. When he looked up at Sophie, he shook his head. "That's not what I see here."

"What do you see?" Sophie said.

Dr. Peter nodded for her to look on with him as he traced the lines in Luke with his finger. "Looks to me like he went home with his parents and obeyed them. And that's how he grew in wisdom and stature and favor with God and men. Women, too, I'm sure."

"What's 'stature?'" Sophie said.

"Height."

"Oh, well, forget that," Sophie said. "I'm underdeveloped." She looked at him from under the brim of her helmet. "Does this mean if I obey my parents I'll actually grow. Maybe need a bra someday?"

She could see that Dr. Peter was trying to smother a smile. "No, I think God's in charge of that," he said.

Sophie looked at the Bible again, and she could feel herself pulling back.

"Talk to me, Loodle," Dr. Peter said.

"I don't think I like this part," Sophie said. "It's like it's saying I have to obey my parents even if they — well, Daddy — doesn't even understand me."

"That's what Jesus did." Dr. Peter pulled out a canteen out of the daypack and offered it to her. "Drink?"

Sophie shook her head. As Fiona would have said, she was completely despondent.

Dr. Peter took a few chugs out of the canteen and wiped his lips with the back of his hand, just like a true explorer, but there was no magic in it for Sophie.

"You're not a happy archaeologist right now," Dr. Peter said.

Sophie pulled off her helmet and handed it to him. "I don't think I want to dig anymore," she said. "Not if this is what I'm going to find out."

Dr. Peter looked her right in the eyes.

"Sometimes I don't like what Jesus is trying to tell me the first time I read it, either," he said. "But if I follow it, it never fails me."

Sophie didn't answer.

"Have I ever steered you wrong, Loodle?" he said.

"No," Sophie said.

"So you'll try it? After all, you and Jesus have a lot in common."

Sophie glared at the Bible. "I wish it gave more details about HOW he did it."

Dr. Peter's eyes twinkled. "Those you'll have to get from him," he said. "So keep on digging."

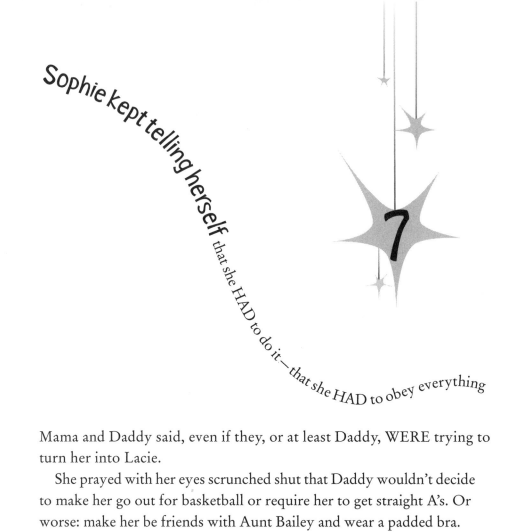

Sophie kept telling herself that she HAD to do it—that she HAD to obey everything

Mama and Daddy said, even if they, or at least Daddy, WERE trying to turn her into Lacie.

She prayed with her eyes scrunched shut that Daddy wouldn't decide to make her go out for basketball or require her to get straight A's. Or worse: make her be friends with Aunt Bailey and wear a padded bra.

That was why it was SO easy to throw herself completely into the excavation of the attic when Wednesday afternoon finally came and she and Fiona and Kitty were gathered in front of Grandma Too's trunk.

They had taken Kitty's suggestion and dressed up like archaeologists. Kitty might not be the best pretender in the Corn Flakes, but she had the best costume.

While Sophie and Fiona were basically in khaki shorts and white t-shirts and floppy hats (Boppa had obviously not forked over for geniuine digging hats), Kitty looked as if she could go to work at Jamestown that very minute.

She had on khaki cargo pants with lots of pockets, and a bright red hard hat — a real one — and hiking boots. The best part was the canvas vest with zippered pockets that held everything, including a neat little pad, a pencil, and a pair of glasses with the magnifiers attached to them.

"Where did you get all this cool stuff?" Fiona said.

"My daddy took me shopping," she said. "We went to that sporting goods store at the mall."

"Wow," Sophie said. She couldn't keep the envy out of her voice.

"Even my Boppa doesn't spoil me that much," Fiona said.

"This isn't spoiling," Kitty said. "He hardly ever buys any of us anything unless it's Christmas or our birthday."

Sophie could understand that. There were six girls in Kitty's family.

"He just said he's glad to see me do something with people besides Julia and them," Kitty said, "because all they ever did was put on makeup and call boys and watch PG-13 movies. And make me cry."

"Are you glad you're a Corn Flake now?" Sophie said.

"You guys don't make me cry," Kitty said.

Sophie decided that was good enough for now. They had important work to do.

First Sophie showed them all the things she had pulled out of Grandma Too's trunk and put on her list. Fiona nodded approvingly.

They decided that Grandma Too had had an extraordinary life — though Kitty still didn't understand why a woman would get married in boxer shorts — and that they wanted to know more about her descendants.

"How do we do that?" Kitty said.

Fiona waved an arm over the plastic containers she'd been peeking into. "It's all right here," she said. "In all these photo albums and scrapbooks."

Kitty wrinkled her nose. "That sounds boring to me."

"An archaeologist is never bored," Artifacta informed her. "Even with the most tedious work."

"Huh," said Madam Munford.

"I know what," Sophie said quickly. Then she cleared her throat and adjusted her glasses. "Madam Munford, I suggest that you learn to operate the video camera so that you can record the amazing discoveries as we make them."

"Cool!" Kitty said.

"Do archaeologists say 'cool'?" Fiona said.

"Oh, yes," Sophie said. It was clear they weren't going to transform Kitty into Madam Munford in just one digging session.

So as Kitty examined the camera and climbed all over the attic like a spider monkey taking shots of them, Dr. Demetria Diggerty and Artifacta Allen pored over the infant pictures of dozens of LaCroixs and Castilles, which had been Mama's last name before she married Daddy.

They made a packet for each one and created a sheet to go with the baby picture, on which they described how they thought that child had turned out, based on the documental evidence they were finding. They also lapsed into Sophie and Fiona now and then to try to guess who the babies were before they turned the photos over to read the names on the back.

It took them until late Saturday to go through all the plastic containers, as well as Grandma Too's trunk. By then, they had thirty packets, on everyone from Grandma Too, herself — born in

1916! — to Zeke, and every conceivable cousin, aunt, uncle, and grandparent in between.

As they held up their flashlights to gaze at their work — and Kitty got it all on film — something suddenly struck Sophie.

"Hey," she said. "We don't have a packet for me."

"You musta missed a box," Kitty said.

"No, we didn't," Fiona said in her Artifacta voice. "Our work has been very thorough."

Sophie nodded — as professionally as she could — but her Sophie-self was plunging into a strange place. She sat down on top of Grandma Too's trunk.

"I'm sure your stuff is around here someplace," Fiona said. "You all just moved last summer. Maybe it's in a box in the garage or something. Or maybe it got lost in the moving van." Fiona wiggled her eyebrows. "Maybe we should trace the path of the van and try to find it in a ditch along the road."

Sophie tried to smile, but even her mouth was sagging. It was as if she were seeing right in front of her what she felt so often in her house: that everybody counted but her.

"Hey, I know," Kitty said. She put down the camera and perched on one of the plastic containers. "Maybe you're adopted."

"What?" Fiona said. "I know we're supposed to examine every theory — but that's just — "

"My oldest sister was adopted," Kitty said. "And then, BAM, my parents had five kids of their own."

"Of their own," Sophie said. Her voice sounded dead, even to her.

"No offense, Kitty," Fiona said. "But that is just ridiculous. Sophie's the middle kid. Why would her parents adopt another kid when they already had one, and then HAVE another one — "

"Of their own," Sophie said again.

She was glad when Mama called up the steps that Boppa was there to pick up Fiona and Kitty. She was also glad that Mama and Daddy went to the NASA Christmas party that night, and Lacie was "babysitting," so Sophie could take her piece of pizza up to her room and not eat it in the kitchen.

She tried to dream up Dr. Demetria Diggerty and perhaps have her argue that there was no possible way Sophie was adopted. The physical evidence didn't point to that; people were always saying that she looked so much like Mama.

But Dr. Diggerty refused to co-operate, and Sophie knew she should go to Jesus.

He was kind of adopted, she thought. *God was his real father, not Joseph.*

But his mother—she was his. Every Christmas as far back as she could remember, she'd heard that story—how Mary gave birth to him in the manger. Somebody else didn't have him and then give him away—

Sophie closed her eyes so tightly her forehead hurt. Jesus was there. His eyes were kind. But all she could think of him saying was, "Be obedient to your parents." And it sounded like Dr. Peter's voice.

She wished Dr. Peter were there right then. She had some questions for HIM:

Like—*Do I have to be obedient to people who aren't even my parents—who have been lying to me ever since I was a little kid—even though they're always telling ME I have to be honest? And I always AM!*

Sophie could hear Zeke and Lacie on the other side of the big square hallway in Zeke's room, where Lacie was reading Zeke the five hundredth book so he would go to sleep. She could picture them with their dark thick hair—not like her own wispy brown—and their sharp faces—not like her own elfin look. They were so much alike—and so much like Daddy—

Sophie suddenly bolted from the bed and ran to the corner of her room, where she wrapped her arms around herself and scrunched her eyes tighter and tried to cut off the thought that was filling her up: *No wonder Daddy will stand up for Lacie and not me. She's his real kid. And I'm not.*

Sophie knew she was in the land of No-God. And even the picture of Jesus's kind eyes couldn't seem to pull her out.

For the next several days, she pretended she wasn't in NO-God Land, and the only way to do that was to spend every spare moment with the Corn Flakes, developing their babies' stories and finding more information. Fiona brought them a perfect notebook for all the packets. It was purple with plastic daisies and a tab that snapped shut. Sophie knew Boppa had bought it, and she tried not to wish that she could go live with HER grandfather. She really didn't know him —

And besides, if he's Mama's father, then he isn't my REAL grandfather — and Grandma Too wasn't my REAL great-grandmother —

That hurt so much in the middle of her chest, Sophie dove back into their project with double-deep energy.

One of the things that WAS good was that Kitty was getting into it. When she got bored with filming them going through boxes and writing things down, she decided to draw pictures of the babies from their photos, and have them grow up and put them in the situations Sophie and Fiona were describing in their stories.

"You are an excellent artist, Madam Munford," Artifact told her one day before school when they sitting on the stage in the cafeteria behind the curtain, looking through their purple notebook for the thousandth time.

"I am?" Kitty said.

"I suggest that we follow these drawings and our pictures and our stories — "

"Based on our historical findings, of course," Sophie put in.

"Oh, yes — and I suggest we put them all into film form."

"Like a real movie?" Kitty said. Her big blue eyes were the size of dinner plates. Excited dinner plates, if that was possible.

Sophie, however, didn't jump up and hug the idea right away. She drew a circle over and over in the dust on the floor with her finger. "I think we need to do some more digging," she said. "Dr. Demetria Diggerty has more work to do."

The early bell rang, and Kitty scrambled for her backpack. When she was gone, Fiona leaned close to Sophie.

"I know what you're doing," she said.

"What?" Sophie said.

"You want to dig in your attic some more because you're obsessed with being adopted."

"What does obsessed mean?"

"It means you can't think about hardly anything else! And it's lame, Soph! Just because there aren't any pictures of you when you were a baby doesn't mean your parents aren't your real parents!"

Sophie squinted at her, through her glasses, through the dimness. "If it were you," she said, "wouldn't you want to know for sure?"

"I think there are some things you just don't have to know," Fiona said.

Sophie couldn't settle in with that idea, even though it had come from Fiona, who knew almost everything. She was glad it was a Dr. Peter day, so she could at least talk to him about it.

But when Mama came to pick her up that afternoon, she said Mama and Daddy were having a session with Dr. Peter instead.

"You get to go home and relax," she said. "I made snowman cookies today, so you can have all you want. I think it's about time we got into the Christmas spirit around our house. Boppa's watching Zeke over at their house, so you have time to yourself for a while. Just keep the doors locked. You have my cell phone number—"

Mama was rattling on as if she couldn't get control of her tongue. Sophie didn't hear half of it. Once she got over being disappointed that she wasn't going to see Dr. Peter, she couldn't wait to get into the attic by herself and see if she could discover something new.

But it was what she didn't find that made the attic seem darker and darker. There was a box covered in what looked like a baby quilt, pushed back into the corner. Sophie knew they hadn't looked in this one, and her heart pounded as she opened it.

But inside were only two baby books — with things written in them about first teeth and first words and first birthday cakes. One was about Lacie. The other one was about Zeke.

Sophie was about to close the lid on them when she noticed that there were a bunch of pictures scattered in the bottom of the box. She scooped them out and leaned with them against Grandma Too's trunk with her flashlight.

They were all of a little girl, from about two years old until maybe five. She was a tiny thing, with skinny wrists and legs and hardly any hair, but Sophie could tell she wasn't a BABY baby because she was standing up and looking at books and hauling a huge stuffed rabbit that was even bigger than she was.

"That's Harold!" Sophie said out loud.

It was the bunny Mama's father had sent her one Christmas, and she'd had it until they moved from Houston and Mama said she was sure it would fall apart if they tried to pack it. Mama had told her that Sophie had insisted on naming him Harold, after Grandpa, because she'd heard Daddy say when she pulled him out of the wrappings that Christmas, "Why did Harold send her that? It's bigger than she is!"

Sophie shone the flashlight on the photo of her dragging Harold up a flight of stairs.

Then that must be me, she thought. *They did take pictures of me!*

That gave her a sudden burst of energy, and she plowed through the rest of the attic, searching for other boxes they might have missed. But there was nothing.

Sophie sat against the trunk again with the Harold snapshot in her hand. *It's like I didn't even exist until I was two years old,* she thought.

Maybe to them, I didn't.

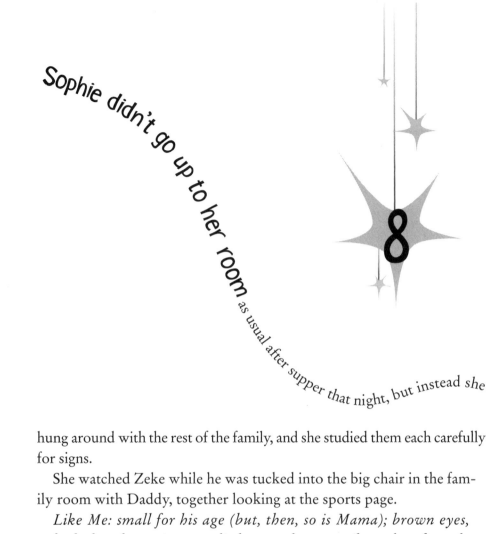

Sophie didn't go up to her room *as usual after supper that night, but instead she*

8

hung around with the rest of the family, and she studied them each carefully for signs.

She watched Zeke while he was tucked into the big chair in the family room with Daddy, together looking at the sports page.

Like Me: small for his age (but, then, so is Mama); brown eyes, only darker than mine; cute little turned up nose (but a lot of people have that).

Not Like Me: dark, thick, coarse hair that sticks up in all directions — like Daddy; half a smile, like Mama; a dimple in each side of his chin, like nobody; and very expressive eyebrows.

Sophie had never noticed that he even listened with his eyebrows. He was such a cute little brother, it made her want to cry.

She also surveyed Daddy as he told Zeke what teams were probably going to be in the Super Bowl.

Like Me: nothing.

Not Like Me: everything.

She moved on quickly to Mama, who was spread out on the couch writing out Christmas cards.

Like Me: light brown hair (like about half the people in the world); brown eyes (like about MOST of the people in the world); petite (because she exercises and she eats like a canary — hello!); high-pitched voice (who wouldn't with three kids?).

Not Like Me: pretty; nice; gets along with Daddy.

It wasn't looking good by the time she went upstairs to observe Lacie. It didn't help that the minute she stuck her head in the door, Lacie said, "If you're going to sit here and look at me like you're doing everybody else, forget it. You're freaking me out."

Sophie switched to Plan B. "No — I wanted to ask you a question."

Lacie got her eyes about halfway rolled, and then she seemed to catch herself. She got up from her desk and flopped down on her bed and patted her mattress.

"Okay," she said. "Have a seat. "I'll tell you anything you want to know."

Sophie could almost hear Daddy telling Lacie she wanted her to be a "role model" for Sophie. She resisted the urge to run out of there with what little of herself she had left, and instead sat on the corner of Lacie's bed.

"I'm not going to bite you," Lacie said. "Here — get comfortable."

She tossed Sophie a pillow shaped like a big fuzzy basketball. Sophie held it in front of her and looked around. It had been a while since she'd been in here. It was hard to "get comfortable" in a room where the walls were covered in huge pictures of women shooting baskets, women making soccer goals, women hitting homeruns. She was a little surprised to see a poster with the Ten Commandments on it tacked to the ceiling over the bed.

"What did you want to ask me?" Lacie said.

"I want to know if you remember when I was first born."

Lacie gave her a blank look. "How would I remember that? I was only two."

"I remember stuff from being two," Sophie said. "I remember getting Harold."

"You remember stories about getting Harold, but you couldn't possibly remember it yourself. I don't even remember you getting Harold, and I was four."

That's probably because you never pay attention to anything I'm doing anyway, Sophie thought.

"So what's the first thing you DO remember about me?" she said.

Lacie didn't linger on it for too long before she shrugged. "I don't know. You've just always been my little sister, as far back as I can remember, which is like when I was five — so you were three."

"You don't remember me being a baby?"

"Unh-uh. I remember Zeke as a baby. He was so precious. He was the first baby I ever got to hold."

"Oh," Sophie said.

"So — is that all you wanted to talk about?" Lacie said. "You don't want to know anything about middle school or boys or anything?"

"Uh, no," Sophie said. "That's all I wanted to know."

She got up and headed for the door.

"You can talk to me anytime," Lacie said. "When you're like this, I can actually have a conversation with you."

"When I'm like what?" Sophie said.

"Like — real."

"Oh," Sophie said again.

As she trudged next door to her own room, she thought, *If this is what being real feels like — it's not what I want to be.*

Sophie had a hard time staying out of No-God Land the next day. It was a heavy, dreary place, but it seemed to hold her within its walls. When at lunch she couldn't even get interested in the Corn Flakes' "Treasures", as they had decided to call the purple notebook, Fiona slapped it shut and said, "We're going to the bathroom."

Sophie followed her there, feeling the stares of the Wheaties behind her. They still sat with the Corn Flakes everyday at lunch, but ever since the day Maggie had brought up the psychiatrist thing, it was as if they were just there to observe, like they were window shopping.

In the restroom, Fiona shoved Sophie into a stall and closed the door behind them. Sophie had to sit down on the toilet seat to make room for both of them.

"Okay, you have to stop obsessing," Fiona said.

"I can't," Sophie said. "Not until I know for sure."

"Have you thought about just asking them?"

Sophie shook her head miserably. "They'd probably just lie to me. They've been doing it for nine years."

"Nine?"

"I was adopted when I was two, I think. That's when the pictures start."

"Okay — I am so over this," Fiona said. "I know a way that we can prove that you are NOT adopted."

"How?" Sophie said.

"I saw it on *Law and Order*. It's something about blood types and stuff."

"Blood?"

"We ask Mrs. Utley. If she doesn't know, then she shouldn't be teaching science, is what I say."

Sophie felt herself go as cold as the porcelain potty she was perched on.

"What's the matter?" Fiona said.

"Maybe you're right," Sophie said. "Maybe there are some things we don't really need to know."

"No way — because you aren't going to be okay until you find out. We're going to Mrs. Utley."

When they were finally in science class at the end of the day, Fiona waited until the students were all at work on the solar system assignment, and then she dragged Sophie up to Mrs. Utley's desk.

She grinned at them, all of her chins wiggling happily. "What are you two up to now?" she said.

"Serious question," Fiona said. "How can you use your blood to prove somebody is or isn't your parent?"

Mrs. Utley's chins all stopped moving. "That IS a serious question," she said. She looked closely at both of them before she went on.

"Well," Mrs. Utley said. "A person would have to have his or her own DNA compared to the DNA of the parent in question. You understand that, right?"

"Is it expensive to do that?" Fiona said.

Fiona! Sophie wanted to say. *How am I going to get blood from Daddy?*

"Very," Mrs. Utley said. "Now, blood type, which just about everybody knows about themselves, can't tell you that someone IS your parent, but it CAN tell you if someone ISN'T. There are some blood types that could not possibly come from the combination of two other people's blood types."

"Do you know how to figure that out?" Fiona said.

"Yes," Mrs. Utley said. She was still watching them closely. The chins were very still. "One thing that is very basic is that if, say, you have the same blood type as your mother or your father, then it's

possible that the one with that blood type is your parent — but it doesn't prove it. Beyond that, I would have to know the exact blood types involved." She folded her plump hands on her desk. "Now, do you want to tell me why we're having this conversation?"

"Research," Fiona said. "Thanks."

The minute Sophie brought up blood types at the dinner table that night, Daddy broke into a grin.

"At last — some interest in science! Some project for school, huh?"

Sophie didn't have time to deny it. Daddy was already going around the table, pointing.

"Your mother is A positive. Zeke is A positive. Lacie is A negative — "

"I've always been special," Lacie said, flashing a cheesy smile.

"And you, Soph, are AB positive. I know that for sure, because it's the same as mine."

"And a good thing, too," Mama said.

"Why?" Lacie said.

"What's for dessert?" Daddy said.

"I'm not done yet!" Zeke wailed.

Sophie let them argue that out in a blur beyond her as she sorted things through. So Daddy COULD be her father. But Mrs. Utley had said that didn't mean he definitely WAS her father. She was really no closer to knowing than she had been before.

Later she padded downstairs to have Daddy check over her math homework. She got almost to the bottom step, when she heard Mama talking to him. They were sitting at the snack bar, having their decaf and, obviously, a serious conversation. All Sophie heard was Mama saying, "Rusty, I just think it's time she knew."

That was all Sophie had to hear. She crept back up the stairs, clutching her math homework in her sweaty hand.

Sophie didn't even have a chance to tell Fiona and Kitty the next morning before Maggie was suddenly there in the hallway with them.

"I know you said you didn't want to know," she said, without a hi or anything, "but I think you should let me tell you about the rumor that's being spread about you."

Sophie was sure she couldn't carry another thing in her mind. ALL the space, God or No-God, was being taken up with the biggest worry on the planet.

"Why does she need to know it?" Fiona said.

"Because it's getting worse," Maggie said. "And it's going to keep getting worse if Sophie doesn't stop it."

"The only reason it's getting worse for me is because YOU keep bringing it up!" someone shouted, someone who didn't sound like Sophie, but was. "I told you, I DON'T WANT TO KNOW. So leave me alone! Just leave me alone!"

Everyone in the hallway outside the Language Arts room stopped and stared. Even Fiona's jaw had dropped. Kitty was whimpering.

But it was Maggie who looked the most stunned of all. She took a step backward and let the cement look take over her eyes, but not before Sophie saw the flash of hurt go through them.

"I'm sorry," Sophie said. Her voice was already shaking.

"Too bad," Maggie said. "Now you're just gonna have to find out for yourself."

She stomped into the room, passing Mr. Denton on the way.

"Everything all right out here?" he said.

"No," somebody said. "Sophie just pitched a fit, right in Maggie's face."

It was Anne-Stuart reporting. Fiona groaned under her breath.

"As if she gives a rip about Maggie," she whispered.

"Thanks for the update, Anne-Stuart," Mr. Denton said.

He smiled at her until she gave up and went on into the room, followed by B.J. and Willoughby, who looked as if they were about to belch.

"You okay, Sophie?" Mr. Denton said when they were gone.

"Yes, sir," Sophie lied.

The bell rang.

"Take a minute and then come on in," he said, and he closed the classroom door.

Fiona and Sophie were left in the hall.

"You go, girl," Fiona said.

"What?"

"Way to stand up to Maggie. She was pushing way too hard."

"I shouldn't have yelled at her like that."

"Like you had a choice! If you hadn't, she would have kept standing there poking at you until you listened to her stupid rumor. You don't need that, and I was proud of you."

But as Sophie trailed behind her into the classroom, she felt anything but proud. There was no place for feeling good about yourself in the Land of No God.

One thing was sure, though, she decided as the day dragged on with people, especially the Corn Pops, staring at her and whispering behind their hands. She had to ask Mama or Daddy for the truth.

And it certainly wasn't hard to decide which one to go to. Mama might stand behind Daddy on everything he said, but at least she didn't yell.

Sophie worked up to it all day, ignoring the whispers and stares at lunch and during classes and trying to imagine herself talking to Mama. It seemed odd to her that even though she didn't TRY to picture Jesus as she planned her approach, his kind face kept popping up, when she least expected it.

Okay, okay, she told him. *I'll obey whatever they tell me. But I still think I have a right to know.*

She was completely ready when she got off the bus and walked "sedately" as Fiona would put it, up to the back door. The question for Mama was already on her lips when she stepped into the kitchen and found Fiona's Boppa at the sink.

"Hello, little wisp of a girl," Boppa said to her. He was smiling his usual I'm-happy-to-see-you smile, but the eyes beneath the caterpillar eyebrows were sad.

"Where's Mama?" she said.

Boppa put a glass of milk on the snack bar and motioned for her to sit.

"Where is she?" Sophie said. "There's something wrong, I know it."

"There is," Boppa said. "Your mama went to Minneapolis. Her dad — your Grandpa — is very sick. She's gone to see him."

"Is she coming back?" Sophie said.

"Of course she's coming back," Boppa said. "But she's your Grandpa's only kid, and since there isn't a Grandma anymore, it's up to your mama to take care of him."

Sophie looked hopefully into Boppa's eyes. "So am I coming to stay at your house?"

"You know, I'd really like that," Boppa said. "But you kids are going to stay here with your dad. Your mama wants the family together."

"Oh," Sophie said.

And she felt the No-God space grow bigger.

9

AMAZEMENT, she immediately burst into tears.

"Mama can't be gone!" she cried. "I NEED her!"

"Your dad will be home shortly," Boppa said. He looked as if he wished Daddy would walk in the door within the next seven seconds.

"I don't want him! He won't understand!"

Sophie shifted from "amazed" to "absolutely flabbergasted."

Lacie dumped her backpack on the floor and flung both hands up to her face. "I failed my English quiz!"

"You?" Sophie said.

"I read the wrong story! And if I get below a C on my progress report, Coach won't let me play in the next game — and I'm the CAPTAIN!"

"Lacie, I think your father will understand," Boppa said.

"No!" Lacie said. "He'll yell! He'll say I wasn't responsible—"

"Not aware of your surroundings," Sophie said.

"I KNOW! Shut UP!"

Lacie slid down the wall and sat on the floor and sobbed. That woke Zeke up from his nap, and the minute he saw Lacie crying, he started. Sophie was about to escape to the attic in search of Dr. Demetria Diggerty when Daddy walked in with a bag with Chinese writing on it.

He took one look at the two crumpled heaps on the floor, said good-bye to Boppa, and made the three of them sit up at the snack bar, containers in front of them, chopsticks in hand. He stood across from them, leaning on the stove, and said,

"Okay, one at a time. Zeke—you first—you're the loudest." Daddy looked at Lacie. "You think you can hold it in for five minutes?"

Lacie gave a miserable nod.

"What's up, Z?"

"I want Mama!"

"I do, too, pal," Daddy said. "The good news is, she'll be back. The even better news is, this means a lot of McDonald's."

"Every day?" Zeke said.

"Whatever it takes," Daddy said.

Zeke tore into his fortune cookies, and Daddy turned to Lacie.

"Next. What's with the tears?"

Lacie poured out her story, crying all over her chow mein. Although Sophie saw Daddy's face-muscles twitch, he just said, "No problem. I'll talk to your teacher—we'll get it straightened out."

"But when? You'll be at work all day!"

"I'm working at home in the afternoon while your mom's gone. I'll pick Zeke up from kindergarten and be here when you girls

83

get home from school." He straightened up from the stove. "I'm Mama until the real Mama gets back."

Sophie put her chopsticks down. Fried rice suddenly tasted like sawdust.

Sure — you're going to go stand up for Lacie with her teacher, even though her mistake was HER OWN FAULT! she felt like yelling at him. *But you haven't even ASKED me if I have any problems.*

But Sophie decided right then he couldn't help her anyway. He wasn't enough Mama for that.

Which was why the next morning she practically RAN straight from the bus to Mr. Denton's room without looking for Fiona and Kitty. She didn't want Fiona grilling her about whether she had asked about the adoption.

Mr. Denton was grading papers when she arrived, and she tried to skip past him to go back to her locker. There was really nobody she wanted to have a conversation with. But he looked up and smiled at her.

"Sophie!" he said. "Just the person I need to talk to."

Sophie dragged herself back to his desk. "I want to recommend you for the Gifted and Talented Program," he said. "You know, GATE. I need for you to take this letter and application home and have your mom or dad help you fill it out, and then one of them needs to sign it."

Sophie stared at the papers he held out to her.

"Me?" she said.

"Of course, you," Mr. Denton said. "And Fiona. And Kitty."

"Why?" Sophie said.

Mr. Denton leaned back in his chair with his eyebrows scrambled together. "Because you're three of the most creative students I've ever had. You all need to be in GATE. His lips twitched. "Unless you don't WANT to, of course — "

"I do!" Sophie said. "Thank you!"

Suddenly, she could feel her chest going loose, as if some space were opening up in there. Maybe God was coming back...

When Fiona arrived she slipped into the table beside Sophie and went straight to a piece of news.

"The Corn Pops are passing a notebook around to each other," she whispered "They're writing in it."

"What do you think it means?" Sophie said.

"I think it means they're trying to be like US. Theirs isn't purple, of course."

"Of course," Sophie said.

She had an open and light and good feeling, and she couldn't wait to get home that afternoon and show Daddy the application. Maybe it didn't even matter if he was her real dad or not, as long as he was proud of her.

He was at the dining room table with his laptop computer and his cell phone and his electronic organizer. Zeke was at the other end of the table, chowing down on a Happy Meal.

Sophie just put the application in front of Daddy and waited for his face to beam.

But it didn't.

He studied the form and the letter for a long time. With each minute that passed, Sophie could feel her open space closing up again. Finally, she couldn't stand it.

"Aren't you proud of me?" she said.

"I'm happy your teacher thinks this much of you," he said. "And he's right — you're definitely creative."

There was such a huge "but" in his voice, Sophie could almost see it.

"But, Soph," he said, "I'm not sure you're ready for this. I'm not convinced you have the basics down yet."

Sophie stared at him. Her chest was closing in like something was pressing against it.

"You mean, you're not gonna let me do it?" she said.

"I mean I need to think about it," he said.

You just DO that! Sophie wanted to shout at him. *I should have known you would find a reason not to believe in me. You would sure let Lacie do it!*

It occurred to her as she stormed up the stairs to the attic that as far as she knew, Lacie had never even been asked to be in GATE. But that didn't help.

Dr. Demetria Diggerty rested against the closed door of the excavation site and closed her eyes. Master LaCroix was more evil than she had imagined. How was she to fight him? How was she to rise to the top of her career with him forever holding her back?

And then the famous archaeologist opened her eyes, and she lifted her chin. How? How indeed! By refusing to give up. Yes, she must obey him as long as he WAS her master. But what if he wasn't?

Tearing off her coat and rolling up her sleeves, Dr. Diggerty headed straight for the boxes that had not yet been unearthed. There must be some important paper that would tell her what she needed to know.

The sun lowered and slowly turned the site dim, but Dr. Demetria Diggerty dug on, through box after box, poring over papers written in some ancient language too difficult to understand. It was only when in desperation she opened the last box that she found what she was looking for. The moment she read its first line, the document fell from her fingers to the floor —

Sophie stood staring at it. She could hardly see it anymore through the blur of her tears. But she knew she would never forget the only line she had read — the only line she needed to read:

Thank you for your interest in adopting a child.

Sophie couldn't do her homework that night. She wouldn't talk to Fiona on the phone. She told Lacie she felt sick and shouldn't eat dinner.

"She really misses Mama," she heard Lacie tell Daddy. "I think we should just leave her alone."

They did—although Sophie knew she could have been surrounded by a thousand people and she still would have felt alone. She was deep into No-God space, and there was no room there for anyone else.

She got herself up and dressed early the next morning and went out to the bus stop long before it was time to, so she didn't have to say much to Daddy. She tried to imagine what Dr. Diggerty would do, but she realized right away that she didn't want to go there. It was Dr. Diggerty who had revealed all this in the first place. If it wasn't for all the digging into the past, maybe Sophie would never have discovered this heinous thing about her life.

And imagining Jesus? That was out of the question. The minute she brought him to mind, she shut him out. She was mad at him. She was mad at God.

She was pretty much mad at everybody.

The bus was at least warm, and when she got on board, she hurried, head down, to her usual seat. As always, Harley and Gill were sitting in front of her, but they didn't turn around. They seemed to be busy with a green binder that they were both reading from. That was okay with Sophie. She didn't want to talk anyway.

Not even Fiona could console her during the day. Sophie couldn't even tell her what she had found. The words just wouldn't come out of her mouth.

She was headed for the bus that afternoon when Daddy was suddenly there beside her. Sophie froze right inside her jacket.

"I can ride the bus," she said.

"I'm taking you to see Dr. Peter," he said

"It's not my day!"

"It is now," Daddy said.

He wasn't yelling and his face wasn't red and his jaws weren't twitching as he talked about nothing all the way to Hampton. But he didn't ask her why she was sitting there chewing at her gloves and banging her feet against the front of the seat, either. He didn't even tell her why she was going to Dr. Peter's.

And Sophie didn't ask.

It was even hard to talk to Dr. Peter. She wrapped her arms around one of the face pillows and squeezed it and forced herself not to tell him she had found out she was adopted.

What if he already knows? she thought.

Sophie squeezed the pillow hard. That would mean that her Dr. Peter was now lying to her, too, by keeping it from her. That might be the worse thought of all.

"So," Dr. Peter said finally. "Must be tough with just your dad at home. He says you're having a hard time."

Sophie nodded, but she clamped her teeth together so she wouldn't be tempted to blurt out something.

"Wow," he said. "I can feel that anger all the way over here."

She glared at him.

"You mad at your father?"

"Yes," Sophie said, teeth still clenched. "And I'm mad at God, too, so I don't even want to talk about him."

Dr. Peter picked up a face pillow, the one with the wart on the end of its nose. "She's so mad at God, she isn't even speaking to him."

Sophie chewed at her lip and banged her feet against the front of the window seat.

"That's what it's like when you love somebody," Dr. Peter said to the pillow. "You can get so mad at 'em, you can't even talk to them."

"I don't love Daddy right now!" Sophie said.

She chomped down with her teeth again, but not so hard this time. Maybe it would be okay to tell Dr. Peter SOME of it. "I got recommended for GATE," she said, "only HE won't sign the permission paper because he says I'm not ready. He doesn't even know anything about me!"

"Ouch," Dr. Peter said. "That does hurt."

"I know," Sophie said, "and I don't want to talk about it."

"That's fine," Dr. Peter said. "Then why don't I talk for a minute?"

Sophie slouched back against the pillows and watched him form his words in his eyes.

"You say you're mad at Jesus right now, so let me tell you about somebody else. You remember John the Baptist, the one who baptized Jesus?"

"His cousin," Sophie said, before she clamped her mouth shut again.

"Right. John gathered friends around him, like you have, and, just like you, he picked them very carefully." The eyes sparkled. "Not just any old person can be a Corn Flake, right? You have to have imagination and not be all about yourself and be willing to take risks."

Sophie just nodded

"Now, I want you to try to imagine yourself sitting down with John as one of his Corn Flakes. And I want you to think of him saying these words to you. You ready?"

"Sure," Sophie said. It couldn't hurt, even if it didn't help.

"John's friends were asking him if he was upset because suddenly a bunch of people were going to Jesus to be baptized, instead of to him. They wanted to know what was up with that. John was their main man!" Dr. Peter rubbed his palms together. "John told them Jesus was God's Son — the Real Deal — and whoever accepted and trusted the Son got in on everything — a complete life here and a forever life after they left the earth."

Sophie didn't see how this applied to her.

"But—" Dr. Peter said, holding up a finger, "he also told them that the person who avoids and distrusts the Son is in the dark and doesn't see life. To that person, God is just an angry darkness."

Dr. Peter gave Sophie a smile that reminded her of the kind eyes she'd seen in her mind so many times. She fought back the tears that were making her throat tight.

"You've already learned that God loves you, Loodle," he said. "Now that you know that, it's your job to love Him, always, with all your heart, no matter what happens. It's okay to be angry with him, but you can't stop loving him. If you do, all you have is angry darkness."

"No-God space," Sophie said.

Dr. Peter nodded and sat back. Sophie pulled some hair into a moustache under her nose and blinked her eyes hard so she wouldn't cry those tears. Dr. Peter tilted his head at her.

"I haven't seen you do that in a long time, Loodle," he said. "And I think we need to do something about it."

"Like what?" Sophie said.

"Like talk to Jesus, first of all, no matter how mad you are at him. AND talk to your dad, no matter how angry you are with HIM. He needs to at least know how important this GATE program is to you." He wrinkled his glasses up his nose as he watched her. "I would be willing to bet that you didn't try very hard to discuss this with him."

"No," Sophie said. "I went to the attic and turned into Dr. Diggerty."

Dr. Peter grinned. "I love that honesty, Loodle. Okay, so if you can, be that honest with your father, too. Tell him how you feel." He looked at the face pillow again. "What has she got to lose?" he said.

10

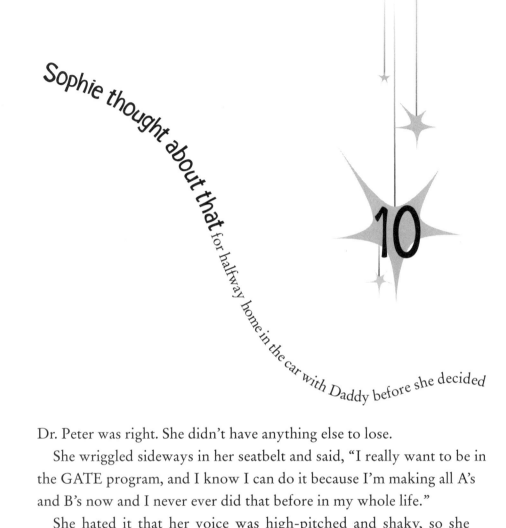

Dr. Peter was right. She didn't have anything else to lose.

She wriggled sideways in her seatbelt and said, "I really want to be in the GATE program, and I know I can do it because I'm making all A's and B's now and I never ever did that before in my whole life."

She hated it that her voice was high-pitched and shaky, so she stopped. She straightened back around and stared at gray Hampton as it turned into Poquoson. There. She had been honest.

"Then here's the game plan," Daddy said. "I'll let you go into GATE, but if your grades drop even a half a point in any subject, I'm pulling you out. Can you deal with that?"

Sophie could only stare at him and nod. The minute she got home, she took the form and a pen to him, before he could change his mind.

But she still didn't feel open and light and good again, even when she put the signed application on Mr. Denton's desk the next morning. When she went back out into the hall to go look for Fiona and Kitty, Anne-Stuart suddenly emerged from the little knot of Corn Pops as Sophie passed and fell into step beside her.

"So you turned in your application," she said.

"How did you know?" Sophie said.

"We saw you come in with it."

Sophie stopped so she could look straight at the sniffly Anne-Stuart. "Are all of y'all in it?" she said.

"Just me and Julia—we got in last year, so we automatically get to apply again."

"Oh," Sophie said.

She tried to move on, but Anne-Stuart grabbed her sleeve.

"I just don't want you to get your hopes up," Anne-Stuart said. "Just because Mr. Denton picks you, doesn't mean you'll get in. OTHER people look at you for OTHER things."

"What 'other things'?" Sophie said.

"Well," Anne-Stuart said, slowly, as if she DIDN'T already know EXACTLY what she was going to say. "They want to find out if you have a lot of problems. Not like with schoolwork, but OTHER problems." She let go of Sophie's sleeve and gave her shoulder a pat. "I just thought you should know that before you got too excited about getting in."

Sophie refused to watch Anne-Stuart as she returned to the waiting Corn Pops. She held her own head high until she was around the corner and had passed through the double doors into the hall that led to the cafeteria. As soon as she knew she was out of sight, she let her shoulders drop, and she made her way somehow behind the curtains on the stage, where she sank to the floor.

She's right, Sophie thought. *I do have problems.*

And Dr. Peter, it seemed, was wrong — because she didn't even want to try to find the God-space right now.

Once again, Fiona, and even Kitty, tried to cheer her up during the day. When science class was over and Sophie was headed out for the bus, Fiona pressed the purple notebook into her hands.

"At least take this home, Demetria," she said. "It will fill the hours."

"I'm not Demetria," Sophie said. "I don't know WHO I am."

But Fiona's gray eyes drooped so suddenly and so far down, Sophie took the "Treasures". She didn't look at it on the bus, though, even when every other girl on there gathered around that same green binder she'd seen Gill and Harley with, reading as if it contained all the secrets of the universe. Nobody invited her to look at it with them, not even the Wheaties, but that was okay. She didn't care.

Daddy made her eat McDonald's with them before she escaped to her room that night. It seemed to her to be cruel and unusual punishment, as Fiona would have said, to have to consume rubber French fries while listening to Lacie gush to Daddy about how wonderful he had been with her English teacher.

"She's letting me retake the quiz!" she said.

"Score," Daddy said. And they high-fived each other.

"May I be excused?" Sophie said.

The minute she was in her room, however, she realized that she'd left her backpack downstairs.

I'm gonna wait until everybody's off doing their thing before I go down and get it, she decided. *I can't listen to Lacie anymore.*

But as she sprawled across her bed, it was hard for Sophie NOT to hear Lacie in her head — because she wanted so much to be saying things like that herself.

Daddy — thank you SO much for standing up for me!

Daddy — you are my hero.

Daddy — you're the best. I mean, the BEST.

Sophie closed her eyes to try to shut it out. Jesus was there, before she even tried to imagine him.

He didn't say anything — of course. Dr. Peter had told her many times that she could only imagine Jesus and talk to him and then wait for him to answer in one of the many ways he did his work.

But his eyes were different this time. They were still kind, but they were also stern — and not like Daddy-stern, just please-listen-to-me firm, the way Dr. Peter's had been that very day.

"Okay," Sophie whispered. "I'll listen."

It was strangely quiet. Even Zeke wasn't banging on something or wailing for Mama. But Sophie didn't hear anything.

I should listen to the Bible, she thought. That was the OTHER thing Dr. Peter kept telling her. Just that day — what was that thing about darkness? Angry darkness . . .

Suddenly, Sophie began to shiver. "I don't want to be in the dark anymore," she whispered. "It's scary here."

She could feel something wet trailing into each ear. "I'm sorry I thought I didn't love You," she whispered. *But I'm so mad — I don't want to be adopted! — I want to have a REAL father who loves me — no matter how mad he is at me.*

Sophie lay there for a long time after that. It got dark in her room. But it wasn't quite so dark inside her.

After a while, there was a knock on the door, and Lacie stuck her head in and snapped on the light.

"Are you okay?" she said.

"Yes," Sophie said She sat up, squinting, and turned away so Lacie wouldn't see the tears.

"I miss her, too," Lacie said.

Sophie started to face her, wanted to say, "Isn't it heinous, Lacie?" But Lacie was already halfway out the door.

"Daddy wanted me to make sure you were doing your homework," she said.

When Lacie was gone, Sophie hauled herself off the bed and scrubbed the tears away with her fists before she put her glasses back on.

I'm going to obey and I'm going to love, she told herself firmly as she went down the steps. *No matter how mad I get.*

When she got to the family room, Daddy was sitting in his chair, thumbing through a book.

It was "Treasures."

That's my private property! she wanted to scream at him. *It's none of your business!*

She reached down, snatched up her open backpack from the floor, and tore back up the stairs. Whether Daddy saw or heard her or not, she didn't know. The next morning, she stalked to the bus stop without the purple notebook.

You're REALLY going to have to help me, Jesus, she prayed. *Because this is MEGA-hard.*

She got to school ahead of Fiona again, and she went straight to her locker. The minute she got there, she knew something was wrong. The door was already partway open.

Sophie pulled it open the rest of the way, and something fell out on her feet.

It was a green binder.

I'm not touching that, Sophie thought. *I know they put it in here so they could say I stole it or something.*

Sophie was tempted to leave it there on the floor, until she saw a bright pink Post-It Note sticking out of the pages. Someone had printed in tidy letters: *SOPHIE READ THIS!*

Sophie picked up the binder and stuffed it into her backpack. Without even saying hi to Mr. Denton, she hurried to the cafeteria stage, parked near a narrow opening in the curtain so she could see to read, and opened the binder.

She scanned the other pages first, and as she read, she could feel her eyes bulging.

There was a page for every girl in sixth grade, even in the other classes. The name was written at the top, and below it, each one in a different colored gel pan, other people had written comments about them. No one had signed any of the comments, but it didn't take a rocket scientist to figure out who had written most of them. Not only was there a bra size written at the top of each page, but most of the comments — except for those about the Corn Pops — were harsh and ugly and heinous.

They said Fiona thought she was all that because she had a lot of money.

They said Kitty was a whiner and a baby and was never loyal to anybody.

They said Vette and Nikki were really boys because all they talked about was cars, and no real girl would do that.

Julia got comments like *she is the prettiest girl in the whole school — and the nicest.*

Anne-Stuart was rewarded with — *totally smart. Smarter than Fiona even THINKS SHE is.*

B.J. — *a friend you can totally count on.*

By the time she had skimmed through the binder, Sophie was terrified to turn to the page marked, *SOPHIE READ THIS!* But there seemed to be a strange pull on her fingers as she turned to the pink Post-It Note. There was no way she couldn't read it.

The first comment was written in ice-blue ink. *Soapie LaCroix is so weerd. We all know she's way behind diveloping — she has NO breasts at all and probly never will. But she's behind-in-the-mind, too.*

In turquoise ink, someone else had picked up the theme. *She has to see a shrink because she's a syko—psycko—crazy.*

The person with the green pen had written: *I used to think it was totally strange that she could be such a freek and her sister Lacey at the middle school could be so totally kewl. But now it makes total sense. She's adopted, and she's too stoopid to know it.*

Sophie was shaking so hard she had to grip the edges of the binder to hold onto it.

But it was the final comment on the page that finally brought her to big, choking sobs. The last girl had written in red: *The only reason her parents adopted her was because they felt sorry for her because somebody left her in a dumpster and she was all shriveled up and her OWN MOTHER didn't even want her. Who DOES?*

Not the GATE program, said the one with the blue pen. She had taken another turn so she could write: *We really need to make sure Mr. Denton and the GATE people know about all this. We DO NOT want her in our program!!!!!!!!!!!!!!!!!!!!!!!!!!!!!*

When Fiona and Kitty found Sophie on the stage, she was crying so hard she couldn't talk. She just handed the binder to Fiona and kept sobbing.

It didn't take long for Fiona to read the Sophie page, with Kitty gasping beside her, and to hurl the whole binder across the stage. It landed with a dusty splash in the corner.

"That is where that trash BELONGS!" Fiona said. Even in the back-stage dimness, Sophie could see her gray eyes blazing as she paced. "All right, I have HAD IT with all of this heinous behavior. First of all, none of that is true, Sophie LaCroix, and I don't want you believing a word of it."

"But I AM flat-chested," Sophie said. "And I DO see a therapist. And I AM adopted."

Fiona stopped pacing. "You know that for sure?"

"I found a paper about it."

"Did you ask your dad about it?"

"I'm waiting for Mama to come home. But I already have the proof."

Kitty sank to the floor beside Sophie and hugged her. Fiona went back to walking back and forth, each step startling up sneezy clouds.

"Okay, so maybe you're adopted," she said, "but your real mother did NOT dump you in a dumpster. Even if she did, how would THEY know that? They're just making stuff up to be their usual heinous selves."

"How did they even know THIS much stuff?" Kitty said, pointing to the offensive binder in the corner.

"They spy, I know they do," Fiona said. "In the bathroom — in the classroom — they're always around." She stopped, hands on hips. "That isn't the point. The point is, they have to PAY."

Kitty looked up at her, eyes fearful. "What do you mean 'pay'?"

"No," Sophie said. She pulled her face away from Kitty's shoulder. "The point is, the next thing they're going to do is accuse me of stealing their binder."

"But you didn't," Kitty said.

"Of course she didn't," Fiona said. "But since when did the truth make any difference to them?"

"So put it back in one of THEIR lockers," Kitty said.

Sophie shook her head. "I don't know any of their combinations."

"But somebody knew yours."

Kitty and Sophie both looked at Fiona. She was standing perfectly still, eyes aglow.

"Nobody knows my combination but you guys," Sophie said. "I never give it out to anybody that isn't a Corn Flake."

Fiona knelt down beside them and lowered her voice to its best revelation-level.

"Then anybody who has ever BEEN a Corn Flake would still have it," she said. "Now, wouldn't she?"

Three heads slowly nodded. And three Corn Flake Mouths said, "Maggie."

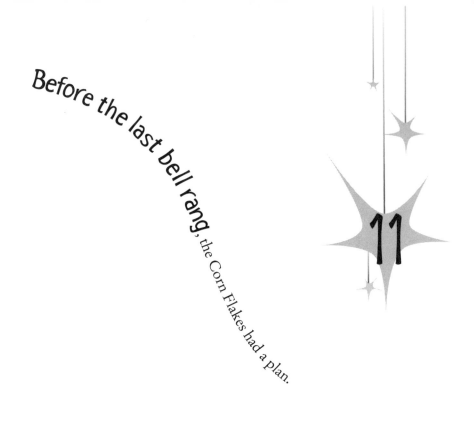

Before the last bell rang, the Corn Flakes had a plan.

11

The first step was to confront Maggie. It wasn't hard to find her, because she was always sitting properly in her seat when the bell rang, sharpened pencil at the ready and the assignment already copied off of the board.

When Mr. Denton said he wanted them to get into groups to work on their story questions, Fiona, Kitty, and Sophie had Maggie surrounded in seconds.

"How many times do I have to tell you?" Maggie said through tight lips. "I don't want — "

"This isn't about what you do or don't want," Fiona said. "It's about what you have to do."

Sophie could tell Kitty was holding back a whimper. That was her only assignment for this first step: not to start crying.

"You put that evil green binder in my locker, Maggie," Sophie said. "And you should help us get it back to where it belongs before the Corn Pops accuse me of stealing it."

"It belongs in the trash," Maggie said. "I was hoping you would throw it away after you read it."

Three pairs of Corn Flake Eyes bulged at her.

"Then why did you make me read it at all?" Sophie said.

"Because you wouldn't listen to me, and I knew they were planning to keep you from getting into GATE."

"Was that the rumor you kept telling us was going around?" Fiona said. "All that stuff they said about Sophie in the book?"

"Why do you even care if I get into GATE or not?" Sophie said. "I thought you hated us."

"I don't hate anybody," Maggie said. Her face set into its usual hard mold. "I'm a good person."

Fiona leaned in, pulling the rest of them with her. "A good person would help us get that binder back to the Corn Pops before they say Sophie stole it." She glanced over her shoulder at the shiny-haired group giggling in the corner. "I'm surprised they haven't accused her already."

"They think I have it so I could write comments about you guys," Maggie said. "I asked them for it."

"Oh," Sophie said.

She glanced at Fiona, who actually looked impressed. "You have more imagination than I gave you credit for, Maggie," Fiona said.

That got a grunt from Maggie.

"Okay, then this is simple," Fiona said. "Since you asked them for it, you can just give it back to them."

"I think you oughta turn them in," Maggie said.

Kitty let go of a whimper.

Sophie shook her head. "Nobody signed their names on their comments," she said. "Even if we took it straight to the principal's office, we can't prove they did it."

"Good thinking, Demetria," Fiona said.

"I thought she was Antoinette," Maggie said.

"I think we should go on with our plan," Sophie said.

"Which is?" Maggie said. The words had stopped thudding.

"We get the binder back to them, and then we go to them as a whole group and we tell them what they're doing is wrong and that we WON'T tell if they promise to destroy it."

"What if that doesn't work?" Kitty said. Her voice was curling up into a whine. "You even said we can't prove they did it."

"I don't think they're smart enough to figure that out," Fiona said.

"I think we're in the right space if we do that." Sophie put out her pinky, and Fiona pinkied with it, and so did Kitty. "Maggie?" she said.

"You want me to do the handshake?" she said.

"It doesn't mean you have to be a Corn Flake," Sophie said. "It just means you're agreeing to the plan."

Maggie stuck her finger like it was a club and hooked it around Sophie's. Then Sophie reached into her backpack and pulled out the green binder. She held it by a corner with two fingers as she passed it to Maggie. Kitty was holding her nose.

Just as Maggie was about to take it in her hands, two other hands reached down, and suddenly the binder was above their heads. Mr. Denton was holding it.

"Why don't I just remove this little distraction so you ladies can get back to work?" he said. "You can pick it up from me after school."

Sophie's heart stopped. Mr. Denton took the binder to his desk and tossed it on top of a pile of papers.

"It's okay — it's okay — " Fiona whispered. "They didn't see."

As Kitty wilted beside her, Sophie glanced back at the Corn Pops who were so into their giggle-fest they didn't seem aware that there was even a classroom around them.

"What if Mr. Denton reads it?" Sophie said.

"Maybe he should," Maggie said.

"But what if he thinks WE did it!" Kitty said.

"Yes, we would so write all those heinous things about ourselves," Fiona said.

"Ladies . . ."

Sophie flipped open her literature book and motioned for everybody else to do the same. Somehow they got through the assignment — and their next two classes — but Sophie knew that for her part it was only because she just kept thinking, *we're still in God-Space.*

Maggie stuck to them like they were all sharing an oxygen mask. She even sat with them at lunch. The Wheaties didn't. They were at another table with their backs to the Corn Flakes.

"What did we ever do to them?" Kitty said.

"I bet the Corn Pops got to them," Fiona said. "But they'll figure it out."

"Speaking of Corn Pops," Maggie muttered.

Sophie looked up to see B.J. approaching. She was obviously on a mission, because her cheeks were the color of two red Christmas balls, and her eyes were narrowed down into slits. She stopped several feet from their table, as if she didn't want to catch something contagious, and slanted the slits at Maggie.

"We have to talk, Maggie," she said.

Maggie didn't even look at B.J. "I got nothing to say."

"Well, I have plenty to say, ladies."

They all jerked around to see Mr. Denton standing at the end of the table. His entire HEAD was red.

"And these are most of the people I want to say it to." He looked at B.J. "If you'll excuse us."

B.J. bolted back to the Corn Pops table, and Mr. Denton sat down next to Fiona, across from Sophie. The rest of the cafeteria went into a low hum.

Without saying another word, Mr. Denton reached inside his tweed blazer and pulled out the green binder. He let it fall to the table in front of him with a thump that went right into Sophie's chest and stayed there.

"It isn't ours, Mr. Denton," Fiona said. "We didn't make it."

"We didn't even write in it!" Kitty said. She was already crying.

"I don't want to think that you did," Mr. Denton said. "I don't want to think that anyone I know took part in this. It's the most appalling thing I've ever read."

"It's definitely heinous," Fiona said.

Mr. Denton nodded. "I can't think of a better word for it. If you didn't create this hideous piece of filth, then who did?"

"Julia, B.J., Anne-Stuart, and Willoughby."

They all looked at Maggie. Each name had thudded to the tabletop next to the binder.

"I know because I saw them doing it, and I got it from them so I could show it to Sophie."

Mr. Denton closed his eyes for a second. "You're telling me the truth?" he said. "No exaggeration? No stretching the facts?"

"That's SO not Maggie's style," Fiona said.

"Julia," Mr. Denton called out without even turning around. "Stop right there."

Sophie watched in amazement as Julia and the other Corn Pops froze halfway to the door. They couldn't have looked more guilty if they had been tiptoeing out of a bank in ski masks with bulging bags.

"Yes, sir?" Julia said.

Mr. Denton turned to look at them. "Over here," he said.

The faces of the Corn Pops behind Julia went white. But the instant Mr. Denton turned back around, Julia gave them all a hard look and fixed a smile on her face. Three more heads came up, three more manes of hair were tossed, and four poster girls for Getting Away with Anything approached the table.

"Sit," Mr. Denton said.

Julia curled her lip. "Where?"

"Down," he said.

The Corn Flakes bunched together so the Corn Pops could gather at the end of the table. Willoughby tried to lean on Julia but she brushed her away. Anne-Stuart sniffed, and B.J. grabbed a napkin and thrust it at her. They all smiled at Mr. Denton in unison.

"What's up, Mr. D.?" Julia said.

Mr. Denton picked up the binder and let it drop again.

All four sets of Corn Pop eyes went to Maggie. She didn't even flinch.

"I understand you are responsible for this," Mr. Denton said.

"Us?" B.J. said. "Are our names on it or something?"

"No, but your handwriting is. I've graded enough of your papers to know it when I see it."

"We didn't — " Anne-Stuart started to say.

But Julia stopped her with the tiniest shake of thick hair. "We aren't the only ones, Mr. Denton," she said. "We would never have thought of doing a Slam Book if they hadn't started it first." She tossed the hair at Sophie and Fiona.

"I don't even know what a Slam Book is!" Kitty wailed.

"She's still such a whiner," Sophie heard Willoughby mutter to Anne-Stuart.

"What do you mean, 'they started it'?" Mr. Denton said. "You're saying there's another one of these floating around?"

"Yes," Julia said. She swept her eyes over the Corn Pops, who all nodded like a panel of judges. "It's purple and they treat it like it's the Bible or something."

"We saw them passing it around to each other," Anne-Stuart said, "and Willoughby said it was a Slam Book."

Willoughby looked a little stricken, until B.J. nudged her with an elbow.

"Didn't you tell your mom about it and she said it sounded like the Slam Books she and her friends used to keep when she was a kid?"

Willoughby gave a poodle-like yip, which Sophie assumed was a "yes".

"That explanation is supposed to clear this up for me?" Mr. Denton said. "You THOUGHT these girls had a Slam Book, so you felt like you needed to start one, too?"

The Corn Pops looked at Julia. Sophie could almost see her fighting under her own skin to somehow come out still being the poster girl. It was almost sad.

"You know what?" Julia said. Her eyes suddenly sparkled with tears. "Ever since we got in trouble for the way we treated Kitty, everybody has been thinking that these girls — " She passed a hand over Fiona and Sophie's heads. "They think these girls are the greatest thing, like, ever — and we're the bad girls all of a sudden." She waved her fingers in front of her eyes, as if she were trying to dry up the tears that Sophie wasn't sure were really there to begin with. "We just thought that if we did what they were doing, everybody would think we were all wonderful, too."

Sophie looked at Fiona. There was an *OH PUH-LEEZE* plastered all over her face.

"No, Julia," Mr. Denton said. "You thought if you could EXPOSE what they were doing, everybody would think they were worse than you are. Wasn't that really the plan?"

"They are!" B.J. said.

While Julia and the others were busy glaring at her, Mr. Denton turned to the Corn Flakes. "Do you have this purple notebook they're talking about?" he said.

"Yes," Sophie said.

"Is it a Slam Book?"

"No," Fiona said.

"May I see it?"

Fiona and Kitty both looked at Sophie. Something began to cave in Sophie's chest.

"It's not here at school," she said.

"That's convenient," B.J. said.

Mr. Denton sliced her off with a look.

"Where is it?" he said.

"At my house," Sophie said.

"Well, the sooner you can get it here, the sooner we can get this whole thing straightened out."

"Can't you just trust us?" Fiona said.

"That wouldn't be fair at ALL," Julia said. She looked expectantly at Anne-Stuart.

"That's right," Anne-Stuart said. "If you read ours, then I think you should read theirs."

"Make her call her mom to bring it over here," B.J. said.

Mr. Denton delivered a glare that should have melted B.J. down like candle wax. "I think I can handle this without your help."

"My mom's not home," Sophie said.

"Also convenient," B.J. muttered.

Sophie looked her squarely in the eyes, so hard that Willoughby shrank back against Julia.

"But my father is home," Sophie said. "I'll call him and maybe he'll bring it over."

Sophie could feel Fiona staring at her. Sophie herself couldn't believe she had just said that. But there it was, and she followed Mr. Denton to the office where they let her call her house. "Daddy?" she said when he answered.

"What's wrong, Sophie?" he said. "Are you sick?"

"No — I just need you to bring that purple notebook to me."

"Were you supposed to turn that in or something?" His voice was starting to get brisk.

"Mr. Denton wants to see it," she said.

Mr. Denton held out his hand. "Let me talk to him," he said.

So Sophie gave him the phone and shrank against the counter while Mr. Denton explained the whole thing.

This better be God-Space, she thought. *Or I'm doomed.*

Mr. Denton said a few "yes, sirs," and handed the phone back to Sophie.

"Daddy?" she said.

"I'm coming over there, Sophie," Daddy said. She could almost see his jaw muscles going into spasms. "And I am NOT happy."

When Sophie's father arrived, Mr. Denton, the Corn Flakes, the Corn Pops,

12

and Maggie were waiting in the conference room in the office.

The minute Sophie saw Daddy, she knew it was all over. His face was purple-red, and his eyes were on fire, and his face was so tight, the muscles couldn't have moved if they'd wanted to.

Before Sophie could even swallow, he spotted her at the table and came straight for her, putting his hands on her shoulders.

Sophie waited to feel his anger sizzling through his fingers. But Daddy's big hands just swallowed her shoulders and stayed there, like pieces of armor.

It didn't occur to her until Mr. Denton said, "Did you bring the notebook, Mr. LaCroix?" that Daddy wasn't carrying anything.

"No, sir, I did not," Daddy said. His voice was too quiet.

"I'd really like to see it — "

"For you to even ask to see it is an extreme invasion of my daughter's privacy, Mr. Denton," Daddy said.

Sophie completely stopped breathing. Fiona stared up at Daddy with her mouth hanging open.

"I was guilty of that myself when I picked it up last night," Daddy went on. "I thought it was a project for school until you called."

"Then it isn't," Mr. Denton said. His face drooped.

"No, it isn't. But it isn't a Slam Book, or whatever you called it, either, I can tell you that." He squeezed Sophie's shoulders. "Do I have your permission to tell him what IS in that book?" he said.

"Yes," Sophie said. She was afraid to say more — in case this was just a dream and she would wake herself up.

"This Slam Book they are suspected of keeping," Daddy said, "is a collection of personal things created by three very creative young women. It is a tribute to the history of our family. There are things in there about my own grandmother that I never knew. It has nothing to do with anyone else here."

Sophie couldn't see Daddy's face, but she could tell he was looking around the table, by the way each Corn Pop was shriveling, one after another.

"If my daughter wants to show the book to you, Mr. Denton, that is her choice. If she decides not to, I will stand behind her."

I will stand behind her.

I will stand behind her.

Suddenly there was so much God-Space, it was all Sophie could do not to climb up on the table, arms spread wide, and dance in it.

Instead, she lifted up her chin. "We don't want to turn our notebook over to you, Mr. Denton." She turned to Fiona and Kitty. "Do we?"

"No," Fiona said.

Even Kitty said, "No, we don't."

"But I do want to say something else," Sophie said.

Mr. Denton had a smile playing at the corners of his mouth as he said, "Please do."

Between Fiona and Kitty's questioning looks, Sophie directed her eyes at the Corn Pops. Julia was still trying to maintain the queenly air, but the rest of the hive looked withered.

"I AM seeing a therapist," she said, "but I am NOT mentally underdeveloped and I DON'T have serious problems — even if I AM adopted." She took a deep breath. "Because I know my dad loves me anyway."

"Indeed he does," Mr. Denton said. "Julia, B.J., Willoughby, Anne-Stuart — stay here. The rest of you may go on to class. Mr. LaCroix, you want to talk this out?"

Daddy nodded — sort of absently, Sophie thought — and then he knelt down in front of her.

"I'm picking you up after school," he said. "I think we need to have a talk."

There was no muscle-twitching. Sophie nodded solemnly.

He's going to tell me the truth now, she thought as she left the conference room — with Mr. Denton saying, "Well, Julia and Anne-Stuart, you realize GATE is out of the question for you now." What Daddy was going to say wasn't going to be what she wanted to hear — but it didn't mater now. It really didn't. Because Daddy had just stood up for her.

"Sophie?"

Sophie turned around to see Kitty, hanging next to the water fountain.

"We have to get to class," Sophie said.

"I just wanted to tell you something."

"Okay," Sophie said, "but hurry."

Kitty latched both hands around Sophie's arm. "I have to tell you that all this time I've been staying with you and Fiona and pretending to be a Corn Flake because I didn't want to be by myself. But now I really want to be one." She clung harder to Sophie's arm. "I'm proud to be one."

Sophie could feel her wisp of a smile floating onto her face. They had Kitty now, and it was for real. Now, if only Maggie —

"Oh, I'm supposed to give you this."

Kitty dug her hand into the pocket of her embroidered jeans and pulled out a bright pink piece of paper. For a second it made Sophie shiver, until she opened it and saw the same neat printing that had turned the world upside down.

I WANT TO BE A CORN FLAKE, it said.

Sophie hugged the God-Space to her all afternoon. She wasn't even afraid when she climbed into the car with Daddy. Not until he said, "We're going over to Dr. Peter's office." Then she began to sink.

"I thought WE were gonna talk," she said. "You and me."

"We are," Daddy said. "But that's not something you and I do so well, Soph. So I asked Dr. Peter if we could talk over there. He won't be with us — he'll just be around in case we need him."

Dr. Peter showed them both into a small room Sophie hadn't been in before. It had a couple of beanbag chairs, and Daddy folded his big self into one of them, and Sophie curled up in the other.

"I have to say this first," Daddy said. "Sophie Rae, you are not adopted. You are Mama's and my biological kid."

"I AM?" Sophie said. "Are you SURE?"

Daddy's eyebrows went into upside-down V's. "Yes, I'm sure! I was there to see you come into the world. I was the first one to hold you."

Sophie was shaking her head. "Then why aren't there any pictures of me when I was a baby?"

"See, Soph this is the part I never wanted to tell you." He suddenly looked very lost. Sophie was pretty sure she knew the feeling.

He scratched both sides of his head. "Before Mama even got to hold you, the doctors took you off to Neonatal Intensive Care. You were so sick, we didn't think you were going to make it through the first day."

"You thought I was going to DIE?"

"They told us you might. You were born two and a half months before you were supposed to be. You were so small and you had so many things wrong with you—you had to fight for your little life."

Sophie sank back into the beanbag and let that information settle itself into her mind. "We almost lost you four or five times before you were even two years old," Daddy said. "We were so wrapped up in keeping you alive, we didn't even think about taking pictures." He let his head sag for a minute. "I didn't want to take your picture that way. I was afraid that if you lived you would see those photographs and you would always think of yourself as a sick kid. You were a fighter, and THAT's how I wanted you to see yourself."

"When did I get better?" Sophie said.

"Right after you turned two, you seemed to turn a corner. We knew you were going to make it then."

"So that's why I'm underdeveloped," Sophie said.

"The doctors say you'll catch up. Besides, your Mama is just a little bitty thing."

Mama.

HER Mama.

Daddy resituated himself on the beanbag, his long legs sprawled on the floor. "I'm still not clear on how you ever got the idea that you were adopted in the first place."

"I saw that paper."

"What paper?"

"The letter to you and Mama — it said 'Thank you for your interest in adopting a child.'"

"Okay, no more attic for you," Daddy said.

"What did it mean?" Sophie said.

Daddy looked up at the ceiling, as if he were visiting a memory of something he hadn't been to in a long time. "When you were about four and we really knew you were going to be okay, things were going so well for our family, that Mama and I decided we wanted to have another kid to share all that with. Only — it didn't happen right away." Daddy shuffled his feet a little. "Anyway, we started looking into adopting and then, bingo, we found out Zeke was on his way."

Sophie's insides were so shaky, she was sure her voice would be, too, when she said, "So Zeke really IS my little brother, and Lacie's really my sister, and Mama's my Mama — "

"And I'm your father." Daddy leaned toward her. Sophie had never seen his face look confused before, ever. "I got the feeling when I was at the school today that it was the first time you believed I loved you. Is that right?"

Sophie could almost hear Dr. Peter saying, *I love that honesty, Loodle.*

She tangled and untangled her fingers for a few seconds, and then she said, "Yes."

Daddy's face didn't turn red. He didn't demand to know where she got such a ridiculous idea. He just nodded. And he blinked. Hard.

"Look, Soph," he said. His voice was thick, like peanut butter. "The reason I'm so hard on you is because I know God has you here for a very special reason, or you would have died. I want to be sure you have all it takes to fulfill His purpose for you. I want you to be physically strong — that's why I push you toward sports. I want you to get a good education — that's why I'm always raising the bar on your grades. I don't want to see you wasting time on things that don't mean anything."

Sophie shook her head. "I don't do that, Daddy."

To her surprise, he nodded. "I think I'm starting to figure that out, Soph," he said.

And suddenly, Sophie figured something out, too. THIS was what it meant when Jesus went home and obeyed his parents and grew up every way he was supposed to. And THEN he did what God put him there to do.

I'm gonna be that obedient, too she decided, then and there. *Even when Daddy doesn't get me, I have to respect him.*

And she had to start right now.

"Daddy?" she said.

"Yeah, Soph?" he said.

"Thank you for standing up for me today."

Daddy's big face broke into a grin so wide, Sophie could see right into his God-Space.

"You were taking a hit for the team," he said. "I had to be there."

And somehow Sophie knew that he always would be.

Glossary

appalling (uh-PALL-ing) totally shocking or almost heinous

archaeologists (ARE-kay-AH-luh-jists) people who study the stuff that people left behind a long, long time ago

artifact (ARE-tih-fakt) something created by people a long, long time ago, like tools or artwork

camisole (KAA-mih-sole) a short sleeveless shirt worn underneath clothes

cardiac arrest (CAR-dee-ack uh-REST) when someone's heart stops beating

clandestine (clan-DEHSS-tin) secret in an almost sneaky way

cower (COW-er) to crouch or shield from something or someone scary

descendants (dih-SEHN-dunts) people who are born after the ancestors, like Fiona is Boppa's descendant

despondent (dih-SPAHN-dunt) feeling totally depressed and hopeless

dignity (DIG-nuh-tee) feeling worthy and like you're important in a way that matters

documental (DAH-kyou-mehn-tuhl) evidence like an artifact, photograph, or recording that can prove something, usually when this evidence has been documented officially in writing

excavate (ECK-skuh-vate) to dig out and remove

flabbergast (FLAA-burr-gaast) to overwhelm with shock or surprise

flux (FLUHKS) the condition of having diarrhea

gavel (GAA-vuhl) a mallet used to gain the audience's attention or confirm a decision was just made

heinous (HAY-nuhss) shockingly mean, beyond rude, or like wicked in a bad way

jeopardize (JEH-purr-dize) to risk or threaten something dangerously

leeway (LEE-way) freedom given to someone else to make mistakes or do something a different way

mutiny (MYOO-tuh-nee) harshly rebelling against authority, like a sea captain or your parents

obsessed (uhb-SEHST) thinking about something way too much

palisade (paa-luhss-ADE) a fence of stakes used to protect a fort from enemies

precedent (PREH-suh-duhnt) something done or said that serves as a model for someone or something that comes afterward, like a set example to follow

sedately (sih-DATE-lee) quietly and steadily, like in a cool, calm way

swellings (SWELL-ings) puffed up larger than normal size, especially like when it's a body part or area of the body

vexation (veck-SAY-shun) the act of troubling or irritating someone or when you're being troubled or irritated by someone or something

faiThGirLz!™
2 corinthians 4:18
No Boys Allowed
Devotions for Girls
Make it happen girl
Take a quiz!
Conquer the green-eyed monster
By Kristi Holl
with Jennifer Vogtlin
Zonderkidz

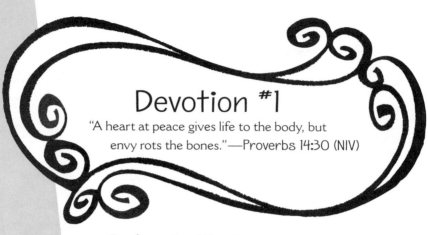

Devotion #1

"A heart at peace gives life to the body, but envy rots the bones."—Proverbs 14:30 (NIV)

The Green-Eyed Monster

A peaceful heart is relaxed and easy, not tense and fearful. This peace of mind and heart will actually give you a longer, healthier life. But envy and jealousy gnaw at you, deep inside. The Bible says it can even rot your bones. That's pretty unhealthy!

Envy and jealousy can take you totally by surprise. You see your dad holding your little step-sister or hugging his new wife. The stab of jealousy can jab hard. Or maybe it's a milder form of envy. You'd give anything for your classmate's designer jeans. Instead, you wear big sister's hand-me-downs and shop at thrift stores.

These are perfectly innocent moments, but how you feel during these times—and what you do about it—is what counts.

Jealousy is sneaky. It's natural to compare ourselves to others or want what someone else has. But when that comparison makes us unhappy, we're probably feeling jealous. Notice how you feel about the good fortune of others: their cool clothes, perfect looks, or their attention in the spotlight. If you feel anything but peace in your heart, you might be feeling jealous. Can you be happy for them instead? Can you compliment them on an outstanding performance or their pretty outfit? Taking positive action is a quick way to kill that green-eyed monster.

The Bible says in James 3:16 that where you have envy (which is another word for jealousy), you will find disorder and every evil practice. Not good! The sooner you tackle these emotions, the easier they are to defeat. God wants you to have a heart filled with peace. A heart at peace is a heart focused on God. So the next time you feel jealous, ask God to help you put jealousy in its place—out of your life!

Did You Know

. . . you can read about jealousy in Genesis 37? When Joseph's half-brothers envied his fancy clothes and were jealous of Joseph's special attention, their evil actions changed history!

More To Explore:

Read James 3:13–18

Girl Talk:

Are you jealous of someone? Be honest with yourself, but more importantly, be honest with God. He will help you overcome jealousy.

God Talk:

Lord, I am really jealous of _____. I know that I shouldn't be, but I am. Forgive me. Please help me to love this person like you do. Thank you for all the good things in my life. Help me to focus on all the blessings I already have instead of envying the blessings of others. And thank you for blessing _____. I know you have more than enough blessings to go around. Amen.

Devotion #2

"What is the price of five sparrows? A couple of pennies? Yet God does not forget a single one of them. And the very hairs on your head are all numbered. So don't be afraid; you are more valuable to him than a whole flock of sparrows."—Luke 12:6–7 (NLT)

Million Dollar Hair

If God cares for small birds that are worth only a couple pennies, then imagine how much more he cares for you. He watches over you so closely that he even knows how many hairs you have on your head. You don't ever need to be afraid. God says you are *valuable*: of great worth, precious, and priceless!

Get outside for a minute. Watch the birds overhead as they glide on the breeze without a care in the world. They aren't worried about where their next worm is coming from! "Look at the birds. They don't need to plant or harvest or put food in barns because your heavenly Father feeds them. And you are far more valuable to him than they are." (Matthew 6:26 NLT) If God provides every need for the birds, how much more will he take care of you?

Thinking deeply about this truth can help when you feel sad and lonely, when you think no one notices you. If he is concerned enough to count every hair on your head, then God is even more concerned about your nightmares, that fight with your friend, your dream of being a nurse, and yes, even your frizzy hair. God—the Creator of the whole universe—cares deeply and personally about *you*.

You are precious to God!

Did You Know

. . . that even David, great king of Israel and close friend to God, felt unimportant and overlooked at times? Read Psalm 13.

More To Explore: Luke 12:22–31

Girl Talk:

Have you ever felt lonely, even if you're around by family or friends? Take a walk in a park, or look through a nature magazine, to remind you that God takes care of everything in this world, including you! It's a perfect time to ask God to fill you with his love.

God Talk:

"Lord, I'm feeling all alone today. I don't know why I'm so valuable to you, but I thank you for your unfailing love. Please help me remember how much you care for me. Amen."

Fun Factoid:

An average head has approximately 100,000 hairs on it. Redheads have about 90,000 hairs. Brunettes have about 110,000 hairs, and blondes have about 140,000 hairs.

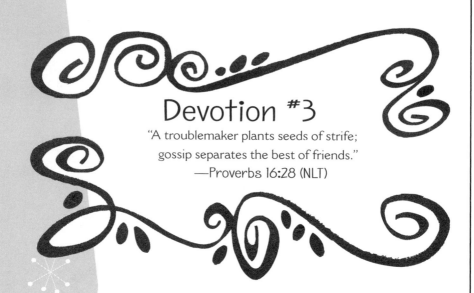

Devotion #3

*"A troublemaker plants seeds of strife;
gossip separates the best of friends."*
—Proverbs 16:28 (NLT)

Tame the Tongue

We all know people who enjoy stirring up trouble by telling people's secrets. Although it's tempting to do this, beware! It can cause a permanent division between even the best of best friends.

You know how it is. Someone whispers that they know Trish's boyfriend is IMing another girl. Or Ms. Gossip tells a juicy tidbit about Alyssa's "F" on the science test. Or maybe you spent the night at your friend's house and overheard a nasty fight between your friend's parents. You're so tempted to repeat it when you're asked how you enjoyed your sleepover. It's especially hard not to gossip about a friend when she's hurt your feelings. We want to tell someone!

Do you want to be known as a troublemaker? No! Gossip hurts others, and it can come back to hurt you too when you lose friends. What's a better choice? "He who covers and forgives an offense seeks love, but he who repeats or harps on a matter separates even close friends." (Proverbs 17:9 NIV)

Instead of repeating someone's private information, zip your lip and sit on it. If you've already gossiped, ask God's forgiveness. Then go back to those you spread tales to and admit you were wrong to gossip. Last, apologize to your friend for repeating a story about her. Next time you're tempted to gossip, "cover and forgive an offense" and keep your friendship close and loving.

Avoid being a troublemaker who stirs up conflict. Instead, control your tongue and tell any "secrets" you know about others only to God. Then pray for that person, like a *real* friend would.

Did You Know

. . . that James, brother of Jesus and author of the book of James, says the tongue is "full of wickedness, and poisons every part of the body"? (James 3:6 LB) Makes you think, doesn't it?

More To Explore:

Psalm 34:13–14; Proverbs 15:4

Girl Talk:

Have you caused strife through gossip lately? What should you do when someone wants to share gossip with you?

God Talk:

"Father, I sometimes tell secrets or repeat information that I shouldn't. I realize this is wrong, and I want to do better. I ask that you keep my mouth in

faiThGirLz!
Faithgirlz!™–Inner Beauty, Outward Faith

Available Now!

Sophie's World (Book 1)
Written by Nancy Rue
Softcover 0-310-70756-0

Available Now!

Sophie's Secret (Book 2)
Written by Nancy Rue
Softcover 0-310-70757-9

Sophie and the Scoundrels (Book 3)
Written by Nancy Rue
Softcover 0-310-70758-7

Sophie's Irish Showdown (Book 4)
Written by Nancy Rue
Softcover 0-310-70759-5

Sophie's First Dance? (Book 5)
Written by Nancy Rue
Softcover 0-310-70760-9

Sophie's Stormy Summer (Book 6)
Written by Nancy Rue
Softcover 0-310-70761-7

Available Now!

"No Boys Allowed" Devotions for Girls
Written by Kristi Holl
Softcover 0-310-70718-8

Available now or coming soon to your local bookstore!

Zonderkidz.

faiThGirLz!
Also from Inspirio

Faithgirlz!™ Frame
ISBN: 0-310-80714-X

Ψ

inspirio
The gift group of Zondervan

Faithgirlz!™ Journal
ISBN: 0-310-80713-1

Faithgirlz!™ Cross
ISBN: 0-310-80715-8

Available now or coming soon to your local bookstore!

Get FREE stuff when you purchase Faithgirlz!™ products!
Find out how easy it is …
Visit **faithgirlz.com** for details—it's the place for girls ages 8–12!!

Zonder**kidz**.

We want to hear from you. Please send your comments about this book to us in care of zreview@zondervan.com. Thank you.

Zonderkidz®

Grand Rapids, MI 49530
www.zonderkidz.com